*The Times of My Life*

# THE TIMES OF MY LIFE

*A Memoir*

## Brent Ashabranner

*Illustrated with photographs*

*Cobblehill Books / Dutton*
*New York*

Library of Congress Cataloging-in-Publication Data

Ashabranner. Brent K., date
  The times of my life : a memoir / Brent Ashabranner.
    p.   cm.
  "Cobblehill books."
  Includes bibliographical references and index.
    Summary: The prolific author describes how his interest in writing
developed as he was growing up in the Oklahoma of the Depression and
chronicles his years after World War II as a government worker in
Africa and a Peace Corps official.
    ISBN 0-525-65047-4
    1. Ashabranner, Brent K., date  —Juvenile literature.
  2. Authors, American—20th century—Biography—Juvenile literature.
  3. United States. Agency for International Development—Officials
  and employees—Biography—Juvenile literature.  4. Peace Corps
  (U.S.)—India—Juvenile literature.  5. Depressions—1929—Oklahoma—
  Juvenile literature.  [1. Ashabranner, Brent K., date.
  2. Authors, American.  3. Peace Corps (U.S.)]  I. Title.
  CT275.A8259A3  1990
  300'.92—dc20
  [B]  [92]  90-40920  CIP  AC

Published in the United States by Cobblehill Books, an affiliate of Dutton
Children's Books, a division of Penguin Books USA Inc.
Designed by Charlotte Staub
Printed in the United States of America  First Edition
10 9 8 7 6 5 4 3 2 1

*Once More, for Martha*

# Books by
# Brent Ashabranner

**In Collaboration with Melissa Ashabranner:**

*Counting America:*
   *The Story of the United States Census*
*Into a Strange Land:*
   *Unaccompanied Refugee Youth in America*

**In Collaboration with Russell Davis**

*Chief Joseph*
*The Choctaw Code*
*Land in the Sun*
*The Lion's Whiskers*
*Point Four Assignment*
*Strangers in Africa*
*Ten Thousand Desert Swords*

# *Contents*

# Author's Note

This book is not intended to be a journey in nostalgia; at least, that is not its primary purpose. It is true that much of what I have written about in the pages ahead happened long before my intended readers—and in most cases their parents—were born. But history is not always something that happened a long time ago and therefore has nothing to do with us now. Some periods of history, no matter when they occurred, are special, and affect what we are doing and thinking now and what we will do and think as long as we live. I have lived through most of the special moments of the twentieth century, and my main purpose has been to write about "the times of my life" and why they are important to everyone today.

The chapters about the Peace Corps are adapted from my book, *A Moment in History*. That book was published twenty years ago, but I find that what I wrote then is still very much what I want to say about the Peace Corps and its formative years.

I want to thank my dear sister-in-law Eva Mae Ashabranner for supplying many of the pictures for *The Times of My Life*. My thanks, also, to my old friend Ralph Booze, who came through with photographs of our boyhood together.

—Brent Ashabranner

*xi*

# The World Didn't End

I was a boy of the Great Depression. By the time I was in fifth grade in 1932, the economic famine that gripped America after the stock market crash of 1929 had spread from coast to coast. Its demoralizing pall still hung over the nation when I graduated from high school in 1939. So I did a large part of my growing up in a time that social historians consider one of the most dismal periods in our country's life. The American dream that everyone willing to work hard could build a good life for himself and his family had turned into a nightmare with fearful speed.

The beginning was not like that. I was born in the town of Shawnee, Oklahoma, in 1921, at the outset of a decade of almost unprecedented prosperity and optimism in America. I think that most people during those years believed that moneymaking opportunities were all around them and that they were going to be very well off, maybe even rich.

I am sure my parents felt that way. Our family was small, just my father, mother, brother—four years my senior—and I, and we had an abundant life. My father was a good phar-

1

macist and always had a good job. My mother inherited oil money, not a fortune, but enough to buy a drugstore, which she and my father bought in 1927. The store was in El Reno, a town of about twelve thousand in central Oklahoma, and El Reno was our home for the next six years.

We lived in a spacious white house in a neighborhood full of kids my age. Neither of my parents had been to college, but my mother was a reader and bought books for my brother and me; we had a full set of the *Book of Knowledge,* which I liked, and a set of leather-bound *Stoddard's Lectures,* books about travels in exotic countries. They were over my young head, but I liked to look at the pictures.

My brother was crazy about horses. My parents bought him a pony when we lived in Shawnee and a pretty little roan when we moved to El Reno; the horse was kept in the one remaining livery stable in town. My mother liked good clothes and jewelry and had both. We had a car, not a high-priced Packard or a Pierce-Arrow but a good, dependable Nash. All considered, we were well off.

That was to change, not only for us but for millions of other American families. By the end of 1932 a frightening number of people had lost their jobs; the exact number was never known, but conservative estimates were that between 12 and 15 million persons who needed work could find none. Eighty thousand businesses failed across the country. Five thousand banks closed their doors permanently, and 10 million people or more lost the money they had kept in those banks. Factories stopped production or cut back drastically. The construction industry ground almost to a halt because few people could afford to buy houses. Farmers suffered more than most as the prices for farm products collapsed on both the United States and world markets. Banks foreclosed on farmers' land; along with the land, farmers lost their animals, their homes.

I did not know most of those things in 1932. That was before the time I paid much attention to newspapers, except for the funnies, as we called comic strips in those days. Home television was still a dream of the future; and although my family had a radio—many families did not in the early thirties—my listening was confined largely to such programs as "Little Orphan Annie" and "Jack Armstrong, All-American Boy," with its rousing theme song, "Wave the Flag of Hudson High, Boys." Another of my favorite programs was "Chief Wolf Paw." The chief had a radio club which a boy or girl could belong to by sending a cereal box top for a badge and the secret club password. At this distance in time, I think I can reveal the password without betraying club confidence; it was Ho-wah-ho-so-wah-ka.

But while I had no understanding of the economic disaster that blanketed the country, I did know, as the twenties turned into the thirties, that something was wrong, seriously wrong. I remember often hearing on the radio a sad song with the plaintive question, "Brother, Can You Spare a Dime?" At the movie theater, in the newsreel that always came before the main picture, I saw city scenes of long lines of people waiting for a free meal at soup kitchens and men selling apples on street corners.

Much closer to home, I remember low-voiced conversations between my father and mother, usually late at night as they sat at the kitchen table. I was aware of those talks only when I woke up and got out of bed for a drink of water or to go to the bathroom, but their nighttime talks troubled me vaguely and made getting back to sleep a little harder.

My mother had a diamond ring that she was very proud

of. One day I noticed that it was missing from her finger; when I asked her where it was, she said she was tired of wearing it and had put it away. The ring never reappeared on her finger; not until years later did I learn that she had sold it to pay for medicine and other goods the drugstore had to have but for which my father could not get a bank loan.

In the summer of 1932, my parents lost the drugstore. With business at an all-time low, they could not keep the store supplied with new merchandise. They sold the store, as I recall, to a group of investors, and after paying off debts had only a few hundred dollars left, which my father put in the bank. A month later the bank closed its doors, and even that little bit of money was gone.

I burst into tears when my mother told me we had lost the drugstore. She put her arms around me and told me everything was going to be all right. I think I knew that, and I was crying not for myself but for my father. He was a quiet man who had little time to do things with my brother and me, but we loved him, and I knew he loved us. I sometimes went to the drugstore after school and stayed with him until my mother came in the car to bring him home for supper or brought him a plate of food if he couldn't get away.

In those days drugstores usually opened at seven o'clock in the morning and didn't close until eleven o'clock at night. That was the schedule seven days a week, except on Sunday morning when the store opened at eleven. Usually there was another pharmacist working in the store, but the hours were still long, eleven-hour days (and nights) with a day off maybe once a month. The drugstore was a huge part of his life, and I didn't know what he was going to do without it.

Perhaps it is too much to say that everything was all right after that; but the world did not come to an end, no more for us than for millions of other families who lost their jobs, their businesses, their homes, their savings during the Depression. We moved to a smaller house, but it was in the same neighborhood. My father never lost a day's work. The new owners hired him to run the store that had been his, and his pattern of long hours on the job everyday did not change. He was not bitter. Not once did I hear him complain about his bad luck or curse the politicians who had got the country into such a mess. He could still provide a house for his family, and he could still put food on the table. He had a job.

His salary was a hundred dollars a month. I know that because once on payday my mother gave a dollar to a beggar who had a particularly hard-luck story. I think she was immediately upset at her generosity because as she walked away I heard her say to herself, "We just have ninety-nine dollars left." But she was a good manager, and if the quality of our meals fell off or the way my brother and I dressed changed much, I was not aware of it. Only on Sunday nights, from time to time, did Mother seem to feel the need to remind us that we were poor and must be frugal. On those nights our dinners would be mush, milk, and sugar, nothing more. That did not happen often.

Most of the time my neighborhood pals and I did not think about the Depression, at least on a conscious level. During the long, hot summer of 1932 we played baseball and marbles and made roads in our backyards for the small metal cars we bought at Woolworth's for ten cents each. "Keeps" was a marbles game played in a ring drawn in the dirt. You got to keep the other kid's marble if you knocked it out of the ring with your marble. I was a terrible shot, and my mother could never understand why my marble supply was always so low. Bud Tucker was by far the best marble player in our neighborhood, and his bag of "glassies" and agates grew to awesome proportions. But Bud's mother discovered his treasure trove and took it away from him. "Keeps" was a form of gambling, and she would have none of it. All our mothers agreed; after that we played marbles "for fun," which meant that we had to give back marbles we won. And that wasn't nearly so much fun, even for a loser like me.

One of our favorite activities was to go to the "jungle," which ran along the railroad tracks a few blocks from our neighborhood. The jungle was an untended swampy area of trees and brush that belonged to the Rock Island Railroad. This was a wonderful place to play "Tarzan" and to act out other African adventures that we had seen in such pictures as Frank Buck's *Bring 'Em Back Alive* and *King Kong*. King Kong may not have been an African gorilla, but that was an unimportant detail.

Reminders of the Depression were never far away, even in the jungle near the railroad tracks or, perhaps, especially there. In earlier years, the jungle had been entirely without people, except for us. By 1932 we frequently saw men in the jungle, boiling coffee in an old tin can, and we would talk with them. Most were from the East, working their way West where winters would be warmer and where they believed jobs might be easier to find.

These were the "tramps" of the Depression, hundreds of thousands of young men who could find no work after high school or even college. They were not homeless in the sense that we know homeless today—people with literally no place to live. In most cases they had left a home where the father was out of work and there were too many mouths to feed. They had left home so that others in the family could have their food and in the desperate hope of finding a job.

Sometimes these young men would ask us to bring them

something to eat. We always did. We would run home and explain that we had met Bill or Steve or Hank who hadn't eaten in two days and had to have food. I can't think of a time that our mothers didn't make up sandwiches, usually peanut butter, and put cookies or fruit into the brown paper bag. We would run the food back to the jungle. It is inconceivable that mothers today would let their young sons play in a woods near railroad tracks, talk to men of the road hanging out there, and take them food. But we never had any trouble; not a single bad thing happened. These were not evil men, just hungry and jobless ones. Our mothers knew that.

The summer of 1932, or perhaps it was '33, was terribly hot and terribly dry, the forerunner of the dreadful years of drought and dust storms that blackened the sky and turned much of our part of the country into a dust bowl. Even boys our age could not help being aware of the growing tension and despair among farmers as they watched their crops burn up and their topsoil begin to blow away. El Reno, like most Oklahoma towns, depended heavily upon agriculture. As one rainless day followed another, our parents sat on their front porches at night, feeling the nocturnal heat, talking about the farm disaster.

And then one day it rained. The midmorning sky darkened suddenly, and the rain came down in heavy sheets. I remember very clearly that four or five of us were playing with our toy cars in Billy Beale's backyard when the rain came. We did not run into his house. Instead, we jumped on our bicycles and rode down the neighborhood street, shouting, doing crazy tricks, deliriously happy as the rain pounded in our faces and soaked our clothes. Although we did not know it, the tension that had been building in the farmers, the town, our parents, had been building in us, and now it was released. Our mothers came out on the porches of our houses. They did not call us in. They watched us and laughed. But the rain was soon gone and did not return, and drought held its deadly grip on the land.

Reading was a joy on which the Depression had no effect. I was an active kid, but I loved to read and I loved books; my mother saw to that. Some of my earliest memories are of her reading fairy tales to me and longer stories such as *King of the Golden River,* which I was especially fond of. I learned to read early and went through the standard fare like the Bobbsey Twins and the Oz books. I went on to Tom Swift and the Tarzan novels and a wonderful series about a boy named Jerry Todd and his pal, Poppy Ott. Even today I remember the Jerry Todd and Poppy Ott books as some of the most delightful reading I ever did. My mother didn't try to direct my reading; she didn't have that kind of background. But she took me to the Carnegie Public Library every week and saw to it that there were always books and magazines in the house. No doubt I could have benefited from more guidance in my reading, but I learned to read for fun. After sixty years reading is still fun.

My brother's name was Gerard, but we always called him Gerad; I have no idea why. We were not very close when I was young because of the four years' difference in our ages. He had his friends and I had mine. Gerard had to give up his horse because there was no money for stable charges and feed, but by that time the loss was not such a great one. When he entered ninth grade, he discovered boxing, a sport he loved and became good at. He trained year-round, running, skipping rope, sparring with anyone who would put the gloves on with him. When he was in the eleventh grade, he won the district Golden Gloves championship in the lightweight division. My mother worried that he might get hurt, but she always drove him to Oklahoma City where the boxing matches were held. My father and I were terribly proud of him.

Despite the difference in our ages, I was one of Gerard's sparring partners simply because of my availability. He would let me swing as wildly and as hard as I wanted to just for the practice of blocking my punches. Occasionally, if I got too wild and reckless, he would slip in a left jab to remind me that boxing is a two-way street.

One day when we were sparring in the backyard, a young black fellow about Gerard's age walked by; I had seen him earlier in the day doing yard work down the street. He stopped to watch us and, when we took a break, told Gerard that he boxed quite a bit "in his part of town." Gerard invited him to put on the gloves, and they had a good workout. The boy's name was Vernon, and after that he came to our house at least once a week to work out with my brother; they were well matched and enjoyed the sparring sessions very much. Once in a while I would spar with Vernon, but, unlike Gerard, he would never lay a glove on me; he would only block my wild swings and laugh.

We learned a good deal about Vernon during the months that he came to our house. His father worked for the Rock Island Railroad as a Pullman car attendant. He had two brothers and three sisters, all of whom were in school, as he was. When he graduated, Vernon planned to enlist in the Army. He intended to save his money and, after his enlistment, go to Langston University, which was the Negro college in Oklahoma. Occasionally, Vernon would bring us a sack of apple fritters that his mother made; they were great.

I still find it hard to believe that Vernon was the first and only black person that I ever got to know even reasonably well until years later when I began to work in Africa. Schools were totally segregated when I grew up, and black people lived in a separate and usually wretched part of town known as "colored town." Housing and businesses were as tightly segregated as the schools. In Oklahoma during the thirties and for many years after that, there was virtually no way that a young white person could get to know a young black person. That was true for most of the rest of the country. I am glad I got to know Vernon, even a little bit.

In the late summer of 1933 we left El Reno and moved to Bristow, a town of about five thousand, forty miles from Tulsa. My father had a job offer from one of the town's two drugstores that he felt he couldn't pass up. He would be making $125 a month.

# Writing: Early Urges and Efforts

**I** tried to write my first story in El Reno, when I was eleven. I had just finished reading an absorbing novel entitled *Bomba the Jungle Boy;* under its spell and unhappy because there were no more Bomba books, I began a story called *Barbara the Jungle Girl.* The thought that a writer should try to be original and should avoid imitating another author never entered my head. All I wanted was more good jungle action; as I recall, I planned for Bomba to rescue Barbara from a hostile African tribe. But after a few pages I was hopelessly bogged down in the plot, and *Barbara the Jungle Girl* was never finished.

That was a beginning, however, and I really never stopped writing after that. I have never been entirely certain why my interest in writing persisted, but I have little doubt that it started—as with Bomba—from a desire to tell stories as exciting and satisfying as those I read. During junior high and my first two years of high school in Bristow, my writing was a mirror of my reading interests. I was hooked on books that had the action set in exotic, faraway places. I read Rudyard

Kipling's novels and stories of India. I practically memorized P. C. Wren's French Foreign Legion novels set in the desert of North Africa: *Beau Geste, Beau Sabruer,* and *Beau Ideal.* I lived every moment of the wonderful travel adventures of Richard Halliburton; I swam the Dardanelles with him, dived into a mysterious Mayan well in Guatemala at night, cut my way through untracked Brazilian jungle. I once spent an afternoon lugging boxes around for the owner of Bristow's tiny bookstore. He offered me any book on the shelves for my efforts, and I picked Alec Waugh's *Hot Countries,* a book about the Caribbean Islands. I lived in a small Oklahoma town, but my reading tastes and my imagination were worldwide.

So was my writing. I wrote stories about jewel smugglers in the steamy Southeast Asian city of Bangkok, of gunrunners in Shanghai, of scientists searching for rare orchids in the Amazon jungle. No matter that I knew nothing about these places except what I read; my imagination was having a great time. I would write these stories at night, sitting at the dining room table. Sometimes when he came home from work late at night, my father would read my stories, written laboriously in pencil on sheets of yellow tablet paper. He always said, "That's a good story," nothing more, but it was enough. I would put each new story in a box under my bed.

One day my father gave me a typewriter. It was not my birthday or Christmas or any other special occasion. He just brought it home after work and said, "This will help you write stories." The typewriter was a secondhand, reconditioned Underwood manual standard; if electric typewriters existed in those days, I knew nothing about them. This machine was beautiful. I was well into a typing course in school and wanted nothing more at that time than a typewriter. I had looked at typewriters in the office supply store downtown, thinking that I might be able to earn some money during the summer and buy one. I was sure I had seen this very typewriter; I remembered that it cost thirty-five dollars. That was a lot of money for my father, and I knew he would have to pay it off a few dollars a month. But he saw my happiness, and I know he was glad he had bought it.

Now I was a real writer. The first thing I did was dig my story about jewel smugglers in Bangkok out of the box beneath my bed, type it, and send it to a magazine called *Argosy* in New York. I had read in *Writer's Digest* how a manuscript should be typed and how a stamped, self-addressed envelope had to be sent with the manuscript. I had also read that *Argosy* paid three cents a word for stories they bought. My story was three thousand words long; I began an impatient wait for my check for ninety dollars.

My story came back from *Argosy* with lightning speed; attached to it was a printed, routine rejection slip saying the editors regretted that my story did not "meet their present needs." Undaunted, I found a story in my box about the sepoys' rebellion in India, typed it, and put it in the mail to *Argosy*. If possible, it came back even faster with the same printed rejection slip.

I had begun to talk writing with Max Marple, the reporter for the *Bristow Daily Record*. He was trying to sell magazine stories, had come close a time or two, and he told me he had always heard that a writer shouldn't be discouraged until he had accumulated enough rejection slips to wallpaper his room. I wasn't discouraged, but typing manuscripts was hard work and took time away from writing new stories. I decided to wait awhile before offering any more manuscripts to New York editors.

My great good fortune in high school was to have teachers who took a special interest in me and my writing. In tenth-grade English Mrs. Arthurs gave me as much freedom as possible in fulfilling assignments with the kinds of things I was interested in writing. She read my stories carefully, took them seriously, praised passages she thought were good, used her red pencil to point out where something wasn't clear or a sentence was awkward. Once she called one of my stories a masterpiece and had me read it to the class. I'm sure it wasn't a masterpiece, but it sounded pretty good when I read it out loud, and a girl I liked very much clapped when I finished. That was the first exposure of my writing to the "public," and it felt good.

Mrs. Arthurs also steered me toward other writers, American writers whose focus was American life as it was being lived right then. Marjorie Kinnan Rawlings' *The Yearling*, about a family in Florida, was one of my favorites. I thought MacKinley Kantor's *The Voice of Bugle Ann*, the story of a hunting dog in the Missouri hill country, was wonderful, and Mrs. Arthurs introduced me to my first John Steinbeck books. Later, for a high school graduation present, she gave me Steinbeck's *The Long Valley*, which contains the story, "The Red Pony." I thought "The Red Pony" was the most beautiful short story I had ever read, and it is still one of my favorites.

In eleventh grade Mrs. Covey encouraged me to write about subjects I knew more about. After the reading Mrs. Arthurs had introduced me to that did not seem like such a strange idea. One of the stories I wrote that year was about a boxer. Boxing actually was a subject I knew a good deal about because my brother, Gerard, had continued to box after we moved to Bristow. In fact, he fought professional fights in Bristow and other nearby towns in a little Depression-era, small town, boxing circuit; it was a form of entertainment that didn't cost anybody much money. Gerard boxed mainly because he loved the sport, but he also made ten or fifteen dollars each time he fought. I went to see his bouts whenever I could, and sometimes, when Max Marple was busy, I covered the fights for the *Bristow Daily Record*.

My story was about a fighter whose ring name was Samson and that was the name of the story. Mrs. Covey liked it and had me work on it until I didn't think I could make it any better. Then she entered the story in the national Scholastic Awards competition for short stories, poetry, and essays sponsored each year by the Scholastic Corporation. "Samson" won fourth prize in the short-story division and was printed along with other prizewinners in a book called *Saplings*.

It was my first published story. When I saw it in the book, I knew as clearly as I have ever known anything that I wanted to be a writer. I have never forgotten Mrs. Covey and what she taught me: write about what you know about. And I have never forgotten the difference she made in my life.

# Becoming Myself

**P**sychologists tell us that the very early years of our lives—when we are three, four, five—are most important in shaping our personalities and in determining what our responses to the world around us will be. I have no reason to quarrel with the psychologists about that, but I have always believed that I began to emerge as a person—the real me, the person I grew to be and am today—during my high school years in Bristow.

Beginning to learn to be a writer was important; so was broadening my reading horizons. Those things were a key part of my growing up, but only a part. I had a number of friends, three of whom I was particularly close to. The things we did together during those years, the way we influenced each other, were as important, or more important, than the reading and writing I did alone.

Without a doubt, my closest friend of all was Bud Booze. He came to Bristow with his family from Golden, Colorado, about the time we came from El Reno. Bud was feisty and had a way of irritating people. Our school, like any other, had a bully or two, and inevitably Bud got into fights with them. They were bigger than he was, much bigger, and Bud came out of the fights the worse for wear, but he always stood his ground. One year Bud wanted us to go out for the high school football team. We weren't even remotely big enough to make the team, and I declined. Bud went out anyway. He played with the scrubs, got knocked around a lot, but stayed with it. By the end of the season the coach put him in some games. I can't say that he starred, but he did all right, and, sitting in the stands watching, I sort of wished that I had gone out.

A popular girl in high school—her name was Frances—found Bud fascinating, and he promptly fell in love with her. Although I had gone out a time or two with different girls, I had not yet acquired a real girl friend. Bud was not comfortable with this. If he had a girl friend, I should have one. I don't know how he engineered it, but I was paired with Ruth, Frances's best friend, on a couple of double dates. I promptly fell in love. The four of us had a great summer, but in the fall I lost Ruth to a star football guard. It hurt, truly hurt. I can still remember the pain. Bud's romance with Frances lasted another stormy six months, and then it too ended. It's odd. Later, Bud started going with Ruth, and I dated Frances a few times. But neither arrangement really worked out, and Bud's and my friendship was strong enough to withstand the stress.

Bud had an imagination as wide-ranging as mine. I can remember winter nights when we sat around his house or mine dreaming up adventures we were going to have in places like Australia, India, and the Congo. We never got to any of those places together, but we did make two summer trips to New Mexico, traveling by Greyhound bus, and had our share of adventure climbing mountains and trying to survive on the small amount of money we had accumulated for the trips. One summer we made the trip money by clearing land of trees and brush, the next summer by doing manual work around the local natural-gas refining plant. These jobs left me with a lasting respect for the men who earn their living through hard physical labor. The trips to New Mexico, my first out of Oklahoma, opened my windows on the world a little wider.

I would do almost anything during those hard times to keep from asking my father for money, especially money for dates. I sometimes did have to ask him, and he always gave it, but I made most of my money by working after school. I delivered newspapers and advertising flyers; for almost a year I was delivery boy for the drugstore where my father worked; I did janitorial work on weekends at the Presbyterian Church, of which my family were members. I did odd jobs for the bookstore owner, but he always paid me in books, which was fine with me.

My other good friends were Ralph Corey and Tom Bulwer. Ralph lived just a few doors from our place and was the first friend that I had in Bristow. He was the fastest reader I have ever known. We often stayed at each other's houses, and some nights we just read. Ralph could read four or five books while I was reading one; I wasn't a fast reader but not slow either. I would accuse Ralph of just flipping through those books, not reading them. But when I talked to him about a book we had both read, he always knew as much about it as I did. With that speed, I think he must have read almost every book in our small public library. His much greater familiarity with books pointed me toward some that I'm sure I never would otherwise have read, books like T. E. Lawrence's *The Seven Pillars of Wisdom* and Dostoyevsky's *The*

*Brothers Karamazov*. Books like that were hard going for me but worth the effort.

But Ralph was more than a reader. He loved to go camping, something I had not done much of, and some weekends even in winter, we would go to the Little Deep Fork of the Canadian River or to a place we just called "the rocks," an unusual formation of sandstone a few miles out of town. Usually Bud Booze and one or two other friends would go with us. Those were good times, cooking over a campfire and talking late into the night, sometimes fishing.

The thing that impressed me about Tom Bulwer, my third good friend, was his intelligence. He made straight A's in school, and I never heard him say anything that didn't make good sense. He received some kind of loan or scholarship for college from a fund put together by local businessmen long before such funds were at all common. I think Tom's parents were poor, but I don't really know. He lived in the country and never invited me to his house. I don't know why. And he never did the kinds of things that Bud Booze and Ralph Corey and I did together, but we were still good friends.

Tom wrote poetry and because of that, I tried to write some, too. Sometimes after school we would go down to a student hangout, drink a Coke, and exchange poems we had written. When I compared mine to his, I didn't like the result. But from Tom I learned to appreciate some of the modern American poets that he liked, especially Robert Frost and Edgar Lee Masters. They were poets who could tell a story, and telling stories was still my main interest.

I came to truly know my brother during the Depression years in Bristow, and I learned lessons in determination and sheer guts from him that served me well in the years ahead.

19

Gerard enrolled as a senior in Bristow High School when we moved from El Reno. The move was much harder for him than it was for me. I had a chance to make friends, get to know teachers, grow up in the town. My brother didn't; he went through twelfth grade, graduated, and was at loose ends. He didn't have any real friends in Bristow, didn't know the town, didn't know what to do. There was no money to send him to college, and neither he nor our parents knew anyone in a college who might try to help him. The best job he could find was mopping the floor and opening boxes of merchandise in the drugstore where Dad worked.

Then one day Gerard announced that he was going to study law. A previous renter had left two law books in the apartment we moved into in Bristow. At some point Gerard started browsing through them and became interested. In the thirties it was still possible to become a lawyer by reading law and passing the bar examination. You wouldn't have a law degree unless you went to law school, of course, but if you passed the state bar examination—the same examination that law school graduates took—you would be issued a license to practice law. You would be a lawyer. The only condition was that you had to do your reading and study in a lawyer's office.

With Dad's help my brother found a lawyer who would let him sit in his office and read his law books. The lawyer was Herbert Arthurs, the husband of my English teacher. He was just starting his law practice. They agreed that Gerard would be a receptionist, answering the telephone, even doing some typing and filing. That would give him a desk to study at and a plausible reason for being in the office. In return, besides the use of his law books, Arthurs would help Gerard develop a plan of study. Gerard made application to the

Oklahoma State Bar Association and submitted a study plan; it was approved.

In the summer of 1935, my brother settled in for three years of study and work in Herb Arthurs' law office. The office was located on the second floor of the bank building, next door to the drugstore where Dad worked. In the mornings Dad and Gerard would go to work together at seven o'clock. That way Gerard could get in two hours of reading before the law office opened at nine.

I don't know how my brother did it. The self-discipline that must have been required to sit there week after week, month after month, reading law books is hard to imagine. And how did he live with the uncertainty he must have felt? In time, he was going to take an examination that had been made out for students who had studied for three years at the University of Oklahoma Law School and at other major law schools around the country. He had no assignments, no tests, no professorial guidance to tell him how he was doing. He just read. How could he possibly know whether he was learning what he would need to know to pass the bar examination?

Dad bought Gerard a book called *Ballentine's Law Quizzer*. It contained questions on the whole range of law—torts, contracts, titles, equities, criminal law, much more—and gave answers to the questions. I spent many nights in the living room of our apartment asking Gerard questions from *Ballentine's;* then we would both try to puzzle out whether he had given the correct answer. On other nights Mother would do the quizzing.

In July, 1938, Gerard went to Oklahoma City to take the bar examination, two days of questions requiring detailed essay answers. The first night he called home to say that he thought he was doing all right but wasn't sure. After the two days he came home and waited. We all waited, afraid to talk about the one thing that was on our minds. And then one day the announcement came: Gerard had passed the bar. He was a lawyer.

In those grim Depression days he pumped gas at a refinery and practiced law on the side. But in time he joined the legal staff of the Shell Oil Company and after that became a senior partner in a distinguished Oklahoma City law firm. Gerard was always just a little sensitive that he didn't have a law degree from some prestigious university. I told him many times he was foolish to feel that way. I would remind him that he had the same credentials as Abraham Lincoln, who had become a lawyer by reading books in a lawyer's office.

During my senior year my class in American Civilization (I believe it was called Problems in American Democracy in those days) got to take over the city government for a day, not for real, of course, but at least to sit in the chairs of the various officials and get a feeling for what it was like. One student was the mayor, another the justice of the peace, and so on. I was cast in the improbable role of chief of police. During the afternoon one of the kids acting as a cop on the street brought to the police station a young black fellow he had "arrested." I guessed the black kid was about my age. The "cop" said the young man had parked his truck over a line, taking up two parking spaces, and he was being brought to the station for this offense.

The real policemen in the station were amused at this arrest. The young black kid had no idea what was going on, no idea why a white kid with a badge had brought him to the station, no idea why a white kid was sitting behind the chief of police's desk. I could see on his face bewilderment, anger, a touch of fear. I, as chief of police, was expected to do something. But all I could think of was that it wasn't right. I went to the white high school. Maybe this kid went to the black high school. Did the black high school kids take part in this running-the-city-government day? Of course they didn't. I wondered why.

I had to do something, so I said I wanted to see where he had parked, and he and I went out of the police station. When we reached his truck, an ancient flatbed, I saw that it was parked ever so slightly over one of the lines. I asked him to move it someplace else. He didn't say anything, just got in his truck and drove away. I felt embarrassed and slightly ashamed as I walked back to the police station.

I couldn't get the experience out of my head, and a few days later I told Tom Bulwer what had happened. He was the only person I felt comfortable with to talk about it. He listened quietly, and he said, "It isn't right." I remembered that was the first thought I had had in the police station.

The next day Tom brought me a book of poems by Paul Laurence Dunbar, a poet I had never heard of. "I found this book last year in a Salvation Army book sale," he said. "You ought to read it."

I did read it that weekend, all of the poems in the book. Paul Laurence Dunbar was a black poet; I had never read anything by a black writer. Many of the poems were about love and sorrow and loneliness, and they were beautiful. I marveled at how similar this black poet's thoughts and feelings were to the ones Tom and I had been trying to express. The difference was that he expressed them as a mature, confident poet; we were still groping.

In 1939 I graduated from high school, along with my friends, and went to work as a cub reporter for the *Bristow*

23

*Daily Record,* helping Max Marple find enough stories to fill the paper. My salary was two dollars a day. But never mind. I had a job and a writing job at that. After my first day, I took a copy of the paper around to the drugstore and showed Dad the stories I had written. He circled each one with a red pencil and showed them to Mr. Whittaker, the owner of the drugstore. I could tell that Dad was very proud.

But my work as a reporter didn't last long. Just ten days after I started at the paper, Ralph Corey called from Stillwater. Somehow he had got a job working in the library at Oklahoma A.&M. College. His call was to tell me that another job had opened up in the library and that if I came over fast I could get it. The job would cover room and board, and it offered me the one chance I might have to go to college. My parents and the publisher of the newspaper said I should go, no question about it. The day after Ralph's call I packed my bag and went to college.

The Depression was still very much a part of life in 1939. The only money I had in my pocket when I left for Stillwater was the twenty dollars I had earned during my short time at the *Bristow Daily Record,* and $2.50 of that went for my bus ticket. But I was happy and excited and confident. I know that my friends Bud Booze, Ralph Corey, and Tom Bulwer faced the future the same way. The thing about it was this: we were young and full of life. We had been brought through the Depression by loving parents who had provided us with good homes. We had had teachers who cared about us. The Depression hadn't depressed us.

That is not to say that the Depression did not put its lasting marks on me and millions like me. Having a good job and a steady income have always been of great importance to me. A number of times in my life I thought about becoming a full-time writer, but my final decision always was to take a job or keep the one I had and write at nights and on weekends. The fact that I had interesting jobs in interesting parts of the world made that decision easier, but the need for job security was always in my mind.

The Depression marked me in other ways. I had only modest amounts of money to invest, and I always chose safe, government-protected investments rather than ones with risks that might have paid much more. I have always avoided more debt that I could easily handle. I am not saying these mindsets that influenced my life were bad. They have worked very well for me. But I have always believed that they had their roots in the Depression.

Just as the Depression influenced the lives of people who lived through it, it has influenced the life of our country. During the New Deal program of President Franklin D. Roosevelt in the Depression years and in years since then, Congress has passed laws aimed at ensuring that the United States will never have another depression. Legislation now restricts stock market speculation in many ways. Bank accounts are insured by the federal government. Farm subsidies—price supports for crops—have become standard protection for farmers; federal government help for disaster areas, such as the dust bowl of the thirties, is now possible. Unemployment insurance now offers some protection against job loss, and welfare for the poor is available in every state. Social Security has made life easier for America's aging population, as has Medicare.

All of these government programs came out of the Depression or were hastened by that time of economic disaster. Today we have "recessions," times when the national economy loses some strength, but the safeguards mentioned above and many others have prevented the return of anything resembling the Great Depression of the thirties. People and governments often seem not to learn from the disasters of history. While there are still serious flaws in providing for the economic well-being of some segments of our population, our country without doubt did learn a great deal from the economic tragedies of the 1930s.

# *Starting Out*

**R**alph hadn't told me everything over the phone. When I arrived at the Oklahoma A.&M. library, I discovered that my job—and Ralph's—was only for the summer. In the fall the regular student workers would return to the library and, unless more positions were approved, there wouldn't be any places for us. But that was three months away, too remote to worry about. I moved into the dormitory, shared a room with Ralph, and enrolled in two summer courses; I don't remember what they were.

What I do remember is the library. I was assigned to the charge-out desk and loved it. Taking request slips from people and finding the books in the stacks was like a game, but mainly there was the thrill of handling scores of books everyday. I am sure the Oklahoma A.&M. library's holdings in those days were very modest compared to some of the great university libraries in the country, but I had never seen or imagined so many books on what seemed to be every subject in the world.

Near the card catalog and the check-out desk were long

shelves containing the latest and best fiction and nonfiction being published in America. Everyday after I put in my quota of hours on the job, I would stand before those shelves, looking at the books, reading a few pages from the ones with the most interesting titles, finally selecting two or three to take back to the dorm. I can't begin to recall all the books I read that summer, but a few come easily to mind: Stark Young's *So Red the Rose,* a beautiful novel of the Civil War; Aldous Huxley's *After Many a Summer Dies the Swan,* which I found troubling, perhaps because I wasn't sure I understood it; Margaret Mitchell's *Gone with the Wind,* the biggest novel I had seen but easy to read. I discovered Hemingway, Fitzgerald, John Dos Passos, Somerset Maugham, and others that I continued to read for years to come. I made C's in the two courses I took that summer because I was too busy reading from the library shelves to pay much attention to the assigned readings for the courses.

Fall arrived, and so did the regular student library workers. No more positions were approved, and Ralph and I were out of jobs. By great good luck I found a job waiting tables at a nice little restaurant called the College Shop. For that work the owners gave me my meals. Since my brother, Gerard, was now supporting himself through work at the refinery and fees from occasional law clients, my parents had a little extra money for the first time in years. They paid my enrollment fees—incredibly small by today's standards—and sent me twenty-five dollars a month. Ralph found a job at another restaurant, and his parents helped him. Tom Bulwer came for the fall semester with his scholarship loan, which covered only the bare necessities. We found a room big enough for the three of us in a rooming house; it wasn't great, but it was cheaper than the college dorm. So we were in college without an extra dime among the three of us. That didn't make any difference; we were there. Bud Booze's parents were relatively well off, and he had gone to the University of Missouri to study journalism.

Enrollment day that first fall semester changed my life profoundly and forever. I was standing in one of the long freshman lines waiting to be assigned an advisor and to select my courses for the semester. Since I was enrolling in the School of Arts and Sciences with the intention of majoring in English, the curriculum for the first semester would be quite standard: freshmen orientation, English, history, mathematics—courses that sounded very much like those I had taken in high school. There was a little choice, but the good stuff—courses in the American and English novel, Shakespeare, Chaucer—wouldn't be open to me until I became a junior and senior.

Standing in line immediately ahead of me was a slender, brown-haired, brown-eyed girl. We began a casual conversation, probably about how slowly the line was moving, but at some point I learned that she was from out-of-state, from Roswell, New Mexico. That interested me because New Mexico was the only place in the world outside of Oklahoma that I knew something about on a firsthand basis. I had, in fact, passed through Roswell twice on my way to the mountain town of Ruidoso, where Bud Booze and I had spent part of two summers. She said that she and her family often went to Ruidoso to escape the heat of the Pecos Valley plain where Roswell was located. She was enrolling at Oklahoma A.&M. because her sister, a junior, was studying to be a dietician in A.&M.'s highly regarded School of Home Economics.

At that point the loudspeaker announced that all persons with last names beginning *N* through *Z* should leave and return at eight o'clock the following day. Persons with names

*A* through *M* were to stay and complete enrollment. For the first time I learned that the name of the girl I had been talking with was Martha White. She started to leave. I, Brent Ashabranner, was expected to stay in line.

A number of times in my life I have had to make fast decisions but none ever faster than at that moment. I don't know how I knew it, but I was sure I wanted to get to know this girl from New Mexico better. I stepped out of line and said to her, "Why don't we get a Coke?"

"What does your name begin with?" she asked.

"*A*," I said, "but I'm tired of standing in line."

Since I had spent the summer at A.&M. I could easily pass myself off as an expert. I took her to a favorite campus hangout for the Cokes, then to the library, where I introduced her to one of the librarians and showed her the wonderful shelves of books. I walked her back to Murray Hall, the girls' dormitory where she and her sister were living. Before I left I asked her to go to a movie the next night, and she agreed.

I wish I could say that I was a super student that first year at Oklahoma A.&M. I wasn't. My grades were okay, a *B* average, which wasn't bad, especially since I was sometimes putting in extra hours at the College Shop. But waiting tables wasn't the problem. The truth is that I wasn't nearly as interested in my courses as I was in the girl from New Mexico who lived at Murray Hall.

Fortunately for my morale, she seemed interested in me, and we spent more and more time together. In her wisdom, the Dean of Women had a rule that all freshmen girls must be in their dormitories by seven-thirty at night every Monday through Thursday. That rule probably saved us academically because we didn't do much studying Friday night through Sunday. On weekends we occasionally went to the "mixers" at Murray Hall where girls who lived there could invite boys for dancing and refreshments, and we might go to a movie if I had any money. Martha knew I was poor and once suggested that she pay her own way, but she saw how much that idea offended me and never made the suggestion again. Mostly we just walked the campus paths and sat on the steps of different buildings and talked about ourselves. By the end of the school year—maybe much before that—we knew we loved each other.

Just as something momentous happened at the start of my freshman year at Oklahoma A.&M., so it did at the start of my sophomore year. After a joyous reunion with Martha, who had spent the summer in Roswell, I discovered that a new professor had come to the college. His name was Thomas H. Uzzell, and he had come solely to teach creative writing. What I read about him in the *O'Collegian,* the college newspaper, made my heart pound with excitement.

He had taught creative writing at Columbia University and New York University. He had written stories and articles for *The Saturday Evening Post, Scribner's Magazine, North American Review, The Saturday Review of Literature,* and a host of other important American magazines. He was a former fiction editor of *Collier's,* an immensely popular magazine of the time, as well as former managing editor of *The Nation's Business.* His book, *Narrative Technique,* was considered one of the best in print about story writing. The names of writers who had studied with him early in their careers read like a literary *Who's Who* of the thirties: Anya Seton, Josephine Lawrence, Gertrude Schweitzer, Blake Clark, Paul Gallico.

I knew I had to get into his class, but there was a major problem. It was open only to carefully selected upperclassmen and graduate students. What chance did I, a first-semester sophomore, have of being accepted? Martha asked, "What can you lose by trying?" In an act requiring more than my usual amount of courage, I made an appointment to see the great man, bundled up a few of my stories, including "Samson," and went to his office. I told him about myself; he did not seem impressed. I left my stories with him and went back the next day for the verdict. Professor Uzzell was not there, but his secretary was. She handed me my stories and said, "You're in the class."

Martha was a sophomore now and no longer confined by the seven-thirty rule. That night we celebrated by eating at a restaurant downtown. The bill brought me to the edge of bankruptcy, but it was a wonderful evening.

I did just enough to get by in my other courses, but I wrote my heart out for Tom Uzzell and worked even harder in his small writing workshop the next semester. He was a wonderful man and a great teacher. I quit my job at the College Shop so that I would have more time to write. I told Mr. Uzzell I had to sell some stories because I was starving.

"Write pulp," he said.

At that time, before television took their place, there were many magazines that printed a certain type of story; there were the detective pulps, the Western pulps, the sports pulps, the science fiction pulps, and others. These magazines were called pulps because they were printed on inexpensive, coarse paper. Such magazines as *The Saturday Evening Post* and *Good Housekeeping* were printed on costly coated paper and were called "slicks." There were many more pulp magazines than slicks, and they used many more stories; the pulps were easier to sell to but paid much less.

I could learn from writing for the pulps, Mr. Uzzell said: constructing interesting plots, keeping a story moving, inventing interesting characters and putting them in situations with plenty of conflict, capturing the reader's attention early. Many well-known novelists and slick writers had started in the pulps, he pointed out. He mentioned Dashiell Hammett, whose famous novel, *The Maltese Falcon,* had first appeared in a detective pulp, and MacKinley Kantor, whose *The Voice of Bugle Ann* had been one of my favorites in high school.

I chose the Western pulps. I was, after all, an Oklahoman, and I had studied Oklahoma history both in high school and college. I had soaked up a lot of knowledge about Western life just by growing up in El Reno and Bristow. I discovered that the Oklahoma A.&M. library had an excellent section of Western Americana, and I started taking out books by the armload. I was not forgetting the lesson I had learned in high school: write about what you know.

My first Western stories came back from the pulp magazines with the same kind of printed rejection slips I had become familiar with in high school. And then one day, instead of getting my story back in my stamped, self-addressed envelope, a letter arrived from Rogers Terrill, the head editor of Popular Publications, a company that published dozens of pulp magazines. He said my story "The Golden Herd" had enough novelty to win a spot in their magazine, *Fifteen Western Tales.* A check for fifty dollars was enclosed. Terrill said he hoped I would send more stories.

When I got over the shock, I called Martha at her dorm and told her the good news. She was so happy I could hear the tears in her voice. I ran to Tom Uzzell's office and showed him the letter. He congratulated me and said, "You'll sell now. Just don't stay in the pulps too long." That night Martha and I ate out again; this time I was not afraid of bankruptcy.

\* \* \*

Another bombshell hit at the end of the semester. Tom Uzzell asked me to be his assistant. He had correspondence students as well as college students, and I would be reading and marking some of the routine exercises and helping him with his correspondence. I would receive a hundred dollars a month for a half day's work five days a week, which would leave me time to take a reduced schedule of college courses.

My good fortune left me positively dizzy. Martha and I decided to get married, and we did, just three months after I started working for Mr. Uzzell. We were young—very young—and had the confidence of youth. The decision to marry was one in which being Depression children did not make us cautious. We rented a tiny apartment, fortunately one with a large closet, which I turned into a writing room. As Tom Uzzell predicted, I continued to sell stories, not many but enough to help us pay the bills. There were plenty of rejections, too, and I tried to learn from them. I made one decision that Martha thought was a mistake. I decided not to enroll in college for my junior year but to work for Mr. Uzzell and spend the rest of my time writing. I knew that dropping out of school might be a mistake, but I wanted to be a writer, and this was my chance.

The terrible war that had begun in Europe while we were still in high school raged on as we went to college and now began our married life. From newspapers, radio, and newsreels, we knew of the might of the Nazi Germany war machine as it ravaged Czechoslovakia and Poland, overran France, and bombed Britain. We slowly grew aware of the mortal peril that European Jews were in.

When I think of those years now, I marvel that I could have been so totally absorbed with writing Western stories. And yet that world across an ocean seemed to us, as to most other Americans, not really to be a part of our world. It is true that President Roosevelt clearly wanted to help the embattled European democracies in every way short of sending troops, but the forces of isolationism were powerful in the United States, especially in the press and Congress. We had been dragged into a European war in 1917, according to their view, and it must not happen again. In the Pacific, the Japanese were making nuisances of themselves, but no one outside of Washington paid much attention to that.

On that Sunday in December, 1941, as Martha and I finished a late lunch and listened to some musical program on the radio, an announcer broke in to say that Japanese airplanes had bombed the United States Naval Base at Pearl Harbor, Hawaii, and that damage to American ships seemed extensive. We had planned to go to a movie that afternoon; instead we listened to the radio the rest of the afternoon and into the night as the grim news came in bit by bit.

The next day President Roosevelt gave his brief, dramatic message to a joint session of Congress which began: "Yesterday, December 7, 1941—a date which will live in infamy—the United States was deliberately attacked by the naval and air forces of the Empire of Japan." The President asked Congress to declare war on Japan and concluded with the prediction that "with the unbounding determination of our people we will gain the inevitable victory."

Congress declared war on Japan within hours of the President's speech. On December 12, Germany, in support of its Japanese ally, declared war on the United States, and the following day Congress declared war on Germany. For the second time in twenty-five years, the United States was involved in a world war.

# Sailor on Land

Japan's sneak attack on Pearl Harbor and Hitler's declaration of war against the United States created a ground swell of support among the American people for the war effort. That support did not falter throughout more than three and a half years of fighting; the first year of cheerless news, as the Japanese overran island after island in the Pacific, seemed only to strengthen America's determination.

A nation that had been crippled and demoralized by the Depression for a decade was suddenly bursting with energy. Factories that had been idle for years began producing again, many of them retooling so they could turn out material needed in fighting the war. Work began in shipyards at a frantic day-and-night pace. As millions of men and women joined the Army, Navy, and Marines, civilian workers who a year earlier couldn't find jobs now had many to choose from. "Rosie the Riveter" became a national symbol of women being drawn into the national work force. Desperately needed farm labor became so scarce that agricultural workers were brought from Mexico under a special government program. Store owners who had suffered for years from slow sales now had only the problem of finding enough goods to put on their shelves; people had money to buy everything merchants had to sell.

Did it really take a war to put America back to work? I am sure it did not, but it did take a sense of national purpose that had been sadly lacking during the Depression years. It took a renewal of confidence that the American people still had the courage, determination, and intelligence of their pioneer forebears to solve unsolvable problems.

Tom Bulwer was the first of our college threesome to go to war. He was accepted into training as a Naval Air Cadet. Ralph Corey applied for training as an Army Air Force bombardier and was accepted. My other Bristow pal, Bud Booze, earned a commission as a second lieutenant in the Army Air Corps. I did not want to leave Martha, but I did want to be a part of the war our country was fighting. It wasn't a desire to be a hero. It wasn't bravery. It wasn't even patriotism in any flag-waving sense, although I felt a duty to do what I could, as did most Americans. More than anything else, it was a feeling of not wanting to be left out. This was the biggest thing that had happened in my lifetime, and I couldn't imagine not being involved in it. And we were all sure America's cause was just. Japan and Germany represented pure evil which had to be destroyed, not only for our own sake but for the sake of much of the rest of the world as well.

I knew, of course, that at some point I would be called to serve in the armed forces. I was twenty years old, and although I was married, we had no children. I was not classified 1A (the first category of men to be called) by my draft board, but when they needed me to fill their quota, they would call me. I did not want to wait to be drafted, which would almost certainly mean serving in the Army. If I volunteered, I could choose my branch of service.

I had read about a new unit of the Navy called the Seabees, which stood for Construction Battalions (the initials CB being the basis for the nickname). U.S. military leaders knew from the beginning that the war in the Pacific was going to be a slow, costly process of winning back islands that had fallen to the Japanese army in the early months of 1942. In swift and savage attacks that had been planned for years, the Japanese took possession of the Philippines, much of the Dutch East Indies, Singapore, New Guinea, Guam, and many, many more islands in the South Pacific.

Creating the Seabees was the brilliant idea of Admiral Ben Morell who foresaw the need for teams of skilled construction workers to go in right behind the beachhead assault troops to build and keep repaired airstrips, docks, roads, fuel tanks, barracks, hospitals, and other necessities for holding onto islands retaken. Enlisting in the Navy and becoming a Seabee appealed to me. Their work sounded crucial to winning the war in the Pacific, and, always thinking about writing, I envisioned seeing the war from a different perspective that would provide material for future stories. I didn't have any construction skills, but I thought some unskilled labor must be needed, and I was sure I could be trained to do something useful.

I volunteered for the Seabees in the summer of 1942 and was accepted. I was assigned the grade of seaman second class, the second lowest grade in the Navy. Why I was not made an apprentice seaman, the lowest grade, I don't know and I didn't ask. I was told that I would receive my orders to report for duty soon.

Four months passed, and the call to report had not come.

I wondered if the Navy had lost my records. Martha enrolled in an intensive, six-weeks-training program at Oklahoma A.&M. in the inspection of aircraft parts. When I left for the Seabees, she planned to get a job, both to help the war effort and to make enough money to survive, which she wouldn't be able to do on my pay as a seaman second class.

In early August the first U.S. offensive of World War II began. The target was Guadalcanal, an island in the South Pacific that few Americans had ever heard of. But the Japanese had taken control of this tiny piece of land in the Solomon chain, and from there could threaten the supply lines between the United States and Australia. That threat could not be tolerated. Before dawn on the morning of August 7, men of the First Marine Division swarmed ashore from landing crafts onto the beaches of Guadalcanal. Thus began a bitter fight for the island that lasted for weeks before the Marines finally prevailed. Early in the fighting the first battalion of Seabees to see frontline duty came ashore with the bulldozers and kept open an airstrip that was under day and night attack from Japanese bombers and warships. The serviceable airstrip played a crucial part in the Marines' ultimate victory. The Seabees were praised for their role in the victory, and I was proud of the outfit I would soon be a part of.

My orders to report came in late November. Martha took a job at the Douglas Aircraft factory in Tulsa, and I went to Tulsa with her for a few days while she settled into a small apartment. Our parting hurt. We had been together almost constantly since the day we met in enrollment line at Oklahoma A.&M. over two years ago. Even during the first college summer vacation, I had gone to Roswell to visit her. We were very young and had everything to learn, but we had learned together during our first year of marriage, a year that had been full of love and fun. Now, like millions of other wartime couples, when we said good-bye at the train station, we had no idea what the future would bring.

The train carried me and hundreds of other recruits to Camp Peary, the Seabee training facility near Williamsburg, Virginia. Martha saved all of the letters that I wrote to her during the war; my first letters from Camp Peary I'm sure sounded like millions of letters written by dazed young recruits as they entered wartime boot camp.

"We arrived at Camp Peary Friday night about ten-thirty," I told Martha in my first letter. "It is a new camp, about one-quarter finished, if that. Also, it has been raining here, and everything is a sea of mud. You will bog down over your shoe tops if you make a misstep from the beaten paths. We finally got to bed about one o'clock and were rousted out for breakfast at four-thirty. The camp is built in two sections about half a mile apart; to get from one part of it where we spent the first night to the other part where the mess hall is, you have to walk through a pine forest. When we went through it at five A.M., it was pitch dark and impossible to stay out of the mud.

"Saturday was a tough day. We had another physical, got all of our clothes and bedding, got all of our stuff stenciled, had our hair cut (you should see me!), tried on our new clothes, and then carried everything to our barracks about half a mile away. Everything is complicated by the fact that thousands of new men are pouring into this camp, so confusion and long waits are just routine—and there is always that infernal mud tugging at your feet. We were kept going from six A.M. until six P.M., and that final half mile carrying a 150-pound pack was no fun.

"I had almost no sleep on the train and only about three hours the night before. All I could think about was sleep.

Well, to top things off, I drew fire watch for four hours from midnight until four A.M.''

Other letters from those first days tell about my being surrounded by mountains of potatoes while on KP duty at the mess hall and of hardly being able to lift my arm after my typhoid shot. The tone of shock and, to some extent, dismay that comes through in those early letters I'm sure reflected the feeling of 90 percent of all recruits in the war. We were taken from loving, familiar homes, and thrust into a strange, rigid new world where a person was not really a person but a number on a dog tag.

Very soon, however, the tone of my letters began to change. My Seabee barracks mates at first had seemed just another part of the alien world I had entered, but quickly I began to find them interesting. "They have lived a different life from me," I wrote Martha, "and I will have a hard time getting to know them, but I will keep trying until I do." Most of them were older than I, in their late twenties or early thirties. They were from the world of skilled blue-collar workers: pipe fitters, welders, electricians, heavy equipment operators, carpenters, plumbers, oil-field explosive specialists, car and truck mechanics, even bricklayers.

Most of what they talked about was over my head, but their enthusiasm for their work and what they were going to do in the Seabees came through very clearly. I was reminded several times during barracks bull sessions that many of these men had been out of jobs and unable to practice their occupations during the Depression years. I'm sure that the prospect of working again at what they were good at, even in a war, fueled their enthusiasm. They took the Seabees motto, "Can Do," seriously.

Fortunately, they did not consider me a misfit. Several of the men in our platoon were avid readers of Western pulp

magazines; by happy chance a magazine with one of my stories in it made its way around the barracks, giving me a
special status. My mates were awed by someone who could
put words on paper and make a story out of them, just as I
was awed by someone who could handle a Caterpillar tractor
or wire a hospital for electricity.

More than anything, as the end of boot camp drew near, I
looked forward to a few days of leave when I would fly back
to Tulsa and be with Martha. I wrote her that I had never
liked Bob Wills' song, "Take Me Back to Tulsa," but that
now it was my favorite. Beyond a reunion with Martha, I
had a growing certainty that I had made the right decision
in wanting to do my service with a Seabee battalion. Perhaps
it was a selfish thought, but I could see myself coming back
from overseas someday with bulging notebooks of story material.

And then one day I was told by the pusher, the petty officer in charge of our boot camp platoon, to report to the
personnel office. Someone on the personnel office staff, ex-
amining records of new recruits, had discovered that I could
type. He had also discovered that I had had two years of
college and, as an English major, could presumably spell
reasonably well and perhaps might even be able to help draft
letters and reports and do other work required by the personnel office.

That was the end of my idea of serving in the Pacific with
a Seabee battalion. I went to work in the personnel office
even before the end of boot camp, and when boot camp was
over I became a part of Camp Peary's "ship's company,"
the men assigned to run the camp. I was at Camp Peary for
two years, all of the time spent in the personnel office. I
worked in a department called Battalion Formation; I helped
do the paper work required in putting battalions together,

and I watched many of them go to "the field," as we called the Pacific. I was still technically a Seabee but far from the kind I had thought I was going to be.

To say that I was unhappy or disappointed at being assigned to Camp Peary's ship's company would not be true, but it was a shock. Suddenly everything was changed, and a new kind of wartime experience began. Martha visited Williamsburg; later, after I was promoted to yeoman second class and we could live on my Navy pay, she moved to Williamsburg. We were fortunate to find a room in the home of an old Williamsburg family, and I was able to come in from Camp Peary every other night. Martha helped our financial situation by taking care of our landlady's invalid mother on the nights I had to stay at the base.

It was fun exploring another part of the United States together. On short leaves and weekend liberties we visited Washington, D.C., Richmond, Virginia, and other nearby Southern cities. We spent one magic week in New York City seeing some of the great Broadway plays of that time: *Oklahoma!, Carmen Jones,* and a young Mary Martin in *One Touch of Venus.* We went to Billy Rose's Diamond Horseshoe and the Copacabana, two of the big nightclubs flourishing then. I visited Popular Publications and talked to Rogers Terrill, the editor who had bought my first story. And just living in Williamsburg, a restored colonial town, was a delightful experience.

Two things happened during that generally happy time in Williamsburg that brought the reality of war cruelly home to me. One day an envelope arrived from Ralph Corey. Inside was a letter telling me that Tom Bulwer had been killed in an airplane accident in the Pacific. Ralph enclosed a photograph of Tom in his Naval Air Cadet uniform. Over a year later I received a letter from Ralph's mother with the grim news that he was missing in a bombing raid over Germany; confirmation of his death was not long in coming. Each death stirred old memories and plunged me into a black mood. On both occasions I went to the personnel officer and asked if I could transfer out with a battalion. I'm sure I felt guilty that my friends had died while I was having a safe and in some ways even pleasant war. Each time the personnel officer, an old Navy man, told me the same thing: I was doing the job the Navy wanted me to do. When the Navy wanted to transfer me, it would.

The second time I went to see him, he added, "You'll see more of the field than you'll want to see before this war is over."

# Sailor at Sea

The personnel officer wasn't a bad prophet. A few months after our last talk, Camp Peary's ship's company was substantially reduced, and I was among those transferred out. To my disappointment I was not assigned to a Seabee battalion but rather transferred to the Naval amphibious forces, where I suppose the need for men was greater. The Navy worked in mysterious ways.

Early in 1945 I left Treasure Island, the Navy staging base near San Francisco, on a troopship. As we cleared harbor, the decks were crowded with men chanting, "Golden Gate in '48!" I did not join the chant. Three years seemed to me a pessimistic estimate of how long we would be in the islands of the Pacific before we saw the United States again.

At that time I was a sailor, over two years in the Navy, who had never been to sea. My first letter to Martha (who had returned to her parents' home in Roswell and was working in the post office) describes my shipboard initiation. After telling her about the cheering, laughing men on deck, I wrote, "Two hours later you would have thought that a great plague

45

had struck the ship. We ran into rough water immediately, and it took its toll. Seasickness is a terrible thing because you can't get any relief from it. No matter how sick you get, the ship just keeps rocking and pitching. I was an early victim and was hit pretty hard, but so were about three-fourths of the passengers (not the ship's crew). Scenes of disaster were everywhere. One poor little guy just gave up the fight and collapsed in a dark corner in a semiconscious state. No one gave him a second glance. A big, strapping Marine was stretched limp over a GI can, his head and shoulders inside, making no effort to get himself out. There were dozens of similar cases. After about two hours of tortured wandering around seeking relief from the ship's motion, I finally reached my bunk. Just then an announcement came over the public-address system: 'Prepare to abandon ship.' This, I realized vaguely, was serious, but I thought it might be better just to go down with the ship. I asked the man in the bunk below if I had heard correctly. He said the order was to 'darken' ship, not abandon it. Night had fallen, and we were in water where a Japanese submarine might be lurking. I was almost sorry the order had not been to abandon ship. I did feel a little better in my bunk, however, although I had to hang on all night to keep from being pitched out. The next day the rough weather continued and so did the seasickness.''

On the third day we awoke to a beautiful calm sea, and the nightmare was over. I found my sea legs quickly. During my months in the Pacific I was never again seasick, although more than once my ship was on the edge of a typhoon.

Our troopship stopped for a day at Pearl Harbor and then began the long, stupifyingly monotonous part of our journey. Where we were heading we didn't know, although the hard-working shipboard rumor mill had it that our destination was the Philippines, from where we would be assigned to ships.

We sailed for nine days without sighting an island, a ship, or a plane. We sailed on a sea so calm, so glassy that I kept thinking about Coleridge's ancient mariner, even though we weren't becalmed. The heat during the day was intense but okay on deck at night; and one night, for the first time, I saw the Southern Cross blazing overhead.

Then one morning as I came on deck there was land again. An announcement came over the public-address system that we were passing Guadalcanal. We passed close to the shore, and the hills looked quiet and peaceful. I found it hard to imagine that some of the Pacific war's most bloody battles had been fought here and that the island itself was such a hellhole of disease and tropical miseries.

About two days later we sailed through a narrow strait with the huge bulk of New Guinea on one side of us and the rugged, jagged peaks of New Britain on the other. But it was a small, nameless point of land that fascinated me, the slender cone of a submerged mountain rising perhaps five hundred feet above the water. It was covered with thick tropical growth all the way to the top, and as we passed this tiny island near sundown, there drifted out on a gentle breeze a sweet, pungent odor that I thought must be of ripening bananas and other jungle fruit. This was a scene out of a book by Conrad or Melville. And it was such a wonderful relief from the constant smells of men and greasy cooked food aboard the troopship that I knew this moment would be one of my few good memories from the journey across the Pacific.

Long confinement in a troopship is no fun. It is crowded. The sleeping quarters are hot and stuffy; getting a shower requires endless patience. You live out of your seabag, which contains all your clothes, toiletries, books—everything you possess. Your appetite is almost nil, and what meals you do eat, you eat standing up. But the desire for something cold to drink finally takes hold of you and never lets go. One of my shipboard letters to Martha has this passage: "Whenever you drink anything cold—whether water, milk, or a Coke, just anything cold—think of me and enjoy it for both of us. We have all the water we want; but with so many men drinking at the fountains all day, it always comes out warm. The 'iced' tea served at meals is warm. At times the desire for something cold and thirst-quenching is almost overpowering, and you roam the ship hunting for a fountain that may produce cold water. You never find it."

The rumor was right. We disembarked from the troopship and came ashore in landing crafts on the island of Samar in the Philippines just twenty-five days after we left San Francisco harbor. The station was a new place, hewn right out of the jungle. The receiving "barracks" were tents which held ten men each. You showered, shaved, and brushed your teeth in the same operation under an outdoor shower; there were no mirrors, of course. Mess problems hadn't been worked out; a two-hour wait in line, in the burning sun, for a chance to eat was about average. None of this would have seemed very important, I think, if there had been cold water to drink. There wasn't. It was warmer than it had been on the troopship.

I tried not to gripe; when I did, I felt slightly ashamed of myself. To thousands of Marines and soldiers who had won back these islands from the Japanese, who had spent weeks pinned down on Guadalcanal, Tulagi, New Britain, and all the others we had passed, this receiving station on Samar would have looked like a little bit of paradise.

Nevertheless, when I was assigned to a ship after two

weeks, I left the Samar receiving station without a single regret. My ship was an LST. The initials LST stood for Landing Ship, Tank, but some old hands in the amphibious Navy I talked to said that as far as they were concerned LST meant Large Slow Target. The LST was the workhorse of the amphibious forces in World War II, carrying everything from tanks and other heavy equipment to supplies and troops. Because of its size, the LST was an oceangoing vessel, but its flat bottom allowed it to go right into a beach and discharge cargo from its vast hold.

My LST was part of an old flotilla, and my new shipmates were veterans of a number of island invasions. Some, they said, had been rough, others a breeze. I liked these men immensely; a few were as green as I was, but most of the crew had been in the Pacific a long time and had seen their share of beachhead action. But they were friendly, and from the good-natured horseplay and amicability, they might have been a bunch of guys in a college dorm. There hadn't been any tough invasions in quite a while, they said.

After the troopship and the Samar receiving station, I found the LST very easy to settle into. The quarters were comfortable. We had lockers for storing our gear, and that abominable seabag could be stashed and forgotten. The food was agreeable and plentiful; there was always cold drinking water. The office where I worked was not big, but it was cool and clean. My yeoman's work was dull but a necessary part of the ship's routine: keeping up personnel records, writing transfer orders, keeping inventory records, doing some correspondence. Like everyone else, I had a general quarters assignment or battle station. I was the "hot-shell man" on one of the antiaircraft guns. I wore a pair of gloves that looked like the ones hockey goalies wear, and I was supposed to

catch the ejected shell casing before it banged into the deck.
My record on catches, during rare sessions to make sure the
guns were working properly, was respectable but just barely.

We moved around among the islands of the Philippines,
put into Manila once, got down to New Guinea. We carried
supplies to bases, moved some Australian troops, sometimes
just went from one place or another for no reason that was
apparent to me. During these wanderings I had a chance to
see some of the work the Seabees had done in these islands:
roads carved through jungles, a mangrove swamp converted
into an airstrip, pipelines strung through dangerous coral
reefs so that ships at anchor beyond them could refuel. You
could always tell where the Seabees had been. Marine Corps
Commandant Lieutenant General Thomas Holcomb said that
the Marines had seen the Seabees "performing miracles." I
saw a few of those miracles and was glad I had known some
of the men who had performed them.

In late June we took on a cargo in the Philippines and
sailed for the east coast of Borneo, the biggest island in what
was then called the Dutch East Indies. The Japanese had
occupied Borneo early in the war because of the rich oil fields
around the east coast town of Balikpapan and the refineries
there. This was to be my one amphibious operation of the
war, an assault designed to recapture the oil fields and refineries from the Japanese and further reduce the supply of
precious petroleum for their war machine.

When we arrived in the coastal waters near Balikpapan,
the assault was already well in progress. From miles out at
sea I could see towering pillars of smoke from the burning
refineries. Our planes and the big guns of our fleet had been
pounding the Japanese installations long before we arrived,
and the assault troops had already gone ashore. The beach
had been secured, and the Japanese had been pushed into

the hills above the town. We were at general quarters only once during an alert for an air raid that never materialized. The power of the U.S. forces had simply been overwhelming.

The next morning we beached, unloaded our cargo of vehicles and boxes, and pulled out. But before we left I went ashore and looked around at the devastation that had hit the place. Palm trees were broken, splintered, burned. The ground was pocked with huge shell holes. Balikpapan was almost destroyed, houses burned, buildings wrecked, streets torn up. That was as close as I got to the war.

The relative ease of the assault on Balikpapan made me think, as I had thought many times, about the part chance plays in the life of a person in wartime. The battle for the island of Okinawa had just begun when I arrived at the receiving station in the Philippines. Those awful weeks of fighting on and around Okinawa produced the bloodiest slaughter of the Pacific war. Before U.S. forces would prevail, 103,000 Japanese troops would die; American casualties were over 7,000 dead, 31,000 wounded. At sea the Japanese lost thirty-four ships. More than 4,000 American sailors were killed. If the LST I was assigned to had been ordered north to Okinawa instead of south to Balikpapan, what would have happened?

After Balikpapan we kept moving around, carrying men and equipment, sometimes staying in a port for a week or more, just marking time. The memories of those days are not bad ones: going into a new place with some of your mates just to look around; movies on deck at night with the cool trade winds blowing across the ship; the water slapping against the ship's sides when you're on the move; the bosun's whistle piping down chow; ships in harbor talking to each other with their blinkers; a battleship steaming in, proud and arrogant as if it owned the Pacific and everything in it; the local people coming alongside the ship in their outrigger canoes to trade. All little things but worth remembering.

We knew why we and hundreds of thousands of other Marines, soldiers, and sailors were marking time. In the fall the invasion of Japan itself would begin. No one doubted that. And we had read and heard estimates: over a million American men would die in that invasion. After the battle for Okinawa, those estimates went up.

And then in early August the atomic bombs were dropped on Hiroshima and Nagasaki, and a few days later the Japanese surrendered. The war was over. We were stunned; we couldn't believe it. But it was true, and we began a different kind of waiting—the wait to return to the United States, to be discharged, to be civilians again. A military force of 10 million men and women had to be demobilized, and those who had served longest and in greatest danger deserved to be released first. For me, the wait in the Pacific went on for another six months. I saw the Golden Gate Bridge again in February, 1946.

My war had not been what I thought it would be. I had not been tested in battle, but I had had many of the experiences of war, and I had learned some things that I never forgot.

I learned that it is hard to be objective. The dropping of the atomic bombs was a horrible thing. Over 200,000 Japanese people died. The bomb has made the world vastly more complicated and dangerous. Yet I wonder how many of the one million American men who might have died in the invasion of Japan would have asked President Harry S Truman not to drop the bomb?

Mother and father
as a young couple.

Brent and his brother,
Gerard, about 1925.

Gerard, Vernon, and another friend in El Reno, 1932.

Ralph Booze, Jr., and his grandmother, 1936.

Martha, 1940.

Brother Gerard, 1962, when he was
senior title attorney for Shell Oil
Company, Oklahoma City.

Family group: father, mother, brother, and Brent, Bristow, 1944, while on leave from Camp Peary.

Martha and Brent on a visit to Washington, D.C., 1944. Washington still had streetcars.

Tom Bulwer, a boyhood pal in Bristow. Tom was a Naval Air Cadet, killed in 1943 on a training mission.

The Battalion Formation crew, Camp Peary, 1944.
Brent Ashabranner, back row, fourth from right.

Martha, Brent, and a friend, 1948. They were living in Veterans
Village while working on their degrees at Oklahoma A.&M.

A view of Haik.

Chief priest of the island
monastery of St. Stephen's.

The old storyteller from the
monastery of St. Stephen's.
Russ Davis is adjusting a
battery-run tape recorder.
Russ, an old Marine, always
wore a gun on the trips because
of gangs of bandits. But, in all
of Brent's and his travels, he
never shot at anything but soup
cans.

Martha teaching home economics
at Empress Mennen School, Addis
Ababa, Ethiopia, 1956.

Martha, with Chip, a pet monkey,
in Addis Ababa, Ethiopia, 1956.

Jennifer, age five, and
an Ethiopian friend, 1957.

With a Libyan colleague, Tripoli, Libya, 1959. Photograph by Kenneth W. Skirvin.

Talking with village elder, Libya, 1958.

The Ashabranner family leaving Libya after a two-year stint, 1959.

I learned that our nation, working together with a common purpose, can accomplish almost anything.

I had learned how good the best in American workers could be. So did many others, like Ernest J. King, Chief of Naval Operations. Speaking to the Seabees, he said, "Your ingenuity and fortitude have become a legend in the Naval service."

I learned about the American capacity for adapting. The LST I was on traveled all over the vastness of the Pacific Ocean. In civilian life the skipper had been assistant vice president of a bank; the executive officer had been a high school principal; the communications officer had been a rancher. But we always ended up in the right port.

I learned that war is about sacrifice and sorrow, not about glory and regard. Tom Bulwer and Ralph Corey were my teachers. Almost half a million servicemen and women had given their lives in Europe and the Pacific.

I learned that the world is a big, exciting place.

I learned the importance of a glass of ice-cold water.

## A New America, A New Vision

The United States emerged from World War II with unbounded strength and energy. Its factories were producing at top capacity; the construction industry was booming; the demand for automobiles and all other goods and services unavailable during the war was almost without limit. A feeling of confidence and self-esteem flowed through the country like electricity. Hadn't it achieved victory in the Pacific almost entirely by its own efforts? The United States stood as a towering giant in the postwar world.

By contrast Europe lay prostrate, battered, exhausted, bankrupt from six years of savage war. Factories had been bombed out of existence; roads and bridges lay in ruins; whole cities had been destroyed. Even if Britain, France, and the other European democracies could summon the will to rebuild their shattered countries, where would the money come from?

There was only one answer to that question. If money came from anywhere, it would have to come from the United States. But should the United States involve itself in the affairs of Europe? American statesmen and politicians beginning with George Washington had warned against foreign entanglements. After World War I, President Woodrow Wilson wanted the United States to join the newly formed League of Nations. The President suffered bitter defeat at the hands of an isolationist Congress that refused to approve U.S. membership in that international body. Powerful forces of isolationism continued to dominate our foreign policy throughout the 1920s and 1930s.

World War II transformed United States thinking about its involvement with the rest of the world. In the first place, isolationism had not kept us out of World War II. In the second place, another superpower, the Soviet Union, had emerged from World War II; its political philosophy of Communism quickly presented a challenge to the concept of democracy, not only in Europe but throughout most of the rest of the world. The way to meet that challenge was not to withdraw into "Fortress America." Three hundred years ago the English poet, John Donne, had said, "No man is an island unto himself;" now we were beginning to realize that no nation was an island unto itself.

The first strong evidence of a fresh spirit of American internationalism was our vigorous support for a new world organization to be called the United Nations. The purpose of the organization was to maintain world peace and security and to address economic, social, and humanitarian problems in member countries. Not only did the United States take a leadership role in establishing the United Nations, we became by far the largest financial supporter for the new organization and provided a home for UN headquarters in New York.

The second major U.S. foreign policy initiative, beginning in 1948, was the European Recovery Program, which has

become known in history as the Marshall Plan. A famous
World War II general, George Catlett Marshall was Secretary
of State when he suggested to President Truman a plan of
assistance to aid the recovery of European countries devas-
tated by the war; the aid would be primarily to countries
that were former war allies of the United States but not nec-
essarily limited to them. President Truman supported the
plan and persuaded Congress to endorse it and appropriate
money for it.

The Marshall Plan was spectacularly successful. It has been
called the most successful piece of foreign policy conceived
by any nation in the twentieth century. It was certainly an
astonishing act of national altruism. Winston Churchill called
it the most "unsordid" act in all history. Between 1948 and
1951 the United States poured over $13 billion in aid into
Great Britain, France, West Germany, and a number of other
western and northern European democracies. A large fleet
of merchant ships—150 or more at almost any given time—
carried all kinds of machinery, building materials, drilling
equipment, food, and scores of other commodities needed by
these countries that had lost everything. Within a remark-
ably short time western Europe had achieved a recovery that
would have been unimaginable without Marshall Plan help.

In his inaugural address, after his election in 1948 to a new
term as President, Mr. Truman made a proposal for a program in some ways more visionary than the Marshall Plan.
This, in part, is what he said:

> More than half the people of the world are living in condi-
> tions approaching misery. Their food is inadequate. They are
> victims of disease. Their economic life is primitive and stag-
> nant. Their poverty is a handicap and a threat both to them
> and to more prosperous areas.

For the first time in history, humanity possesses the knowledge and the skill to relieve the suffering of these people.

The United States is preeminent among nations in the development of industrial and scientific techniques. The material resources which we can afford to use for the assistance of other people are limited. But our imponderable resources in technical knowledge are constantly growing and are inexhaustible.

I believe that we should make available to peace-loving peoples the benefits of our store of technical knowledge in order to help them realize their aspirations for a better life . . .

Our aim should be to help the free peoples of the world, through their own efforts, to produce more food, more clothing, more materials for housing and more mechanical power to lighten their burdens.

President Truman's proposal for a bold new program of foreign aid to the poor countries of Africa, Asia, and Latin America struck a responsive chord in the American people and won approval of Congress. The official name of the new federal government program was the Technical Cooperation Administration, but it was soon known everywhere as the Point Four program. The reason for this curious name was simple: the fourth point in President Truman's inaugural address had been his call for a foreign assistance program.

As the 1950s progressed, American technicians in agriculture, health, and education were working in more than sixty developing countries. Beyond any notion of competition with Russia, increasing numbers of Americans were beginning to believe that sharing some of our wealth and knowledge in order to make the world a better place was simply the right thing to do.

# *Africa Calls*

**A**fter the war Martha and I returned to Stillwater and Oklahoma A.&M. College (renamed Oklahoma State University in 1957). My wartime look at the world had convinced me that, whatever I might eventually do as a writer, I needed first to finish my education. A benign government's GI Bill of Rights for World War II veterans helped with educational expenses, and I found a return to writing and selling stories a ready way to supplement our GI Bill income. We lived in the university's "Veterans Village"—a collection of trailers on the edge of the campus—along with hundreds of other married veterans who were starting or finishing their college educations.

I completed my bachelor's degree, switching to secondary education in case I wanted to teach in high school. I followed that with a master's degree in English, my first love. Martha finished her degree in home economics.

Life moved crisply and happily in Stillwater. I was offered an appointment as an instructor in the Oklahoma A.&M. English Department and took it. I continued to sell Western stories but followed Tom Uzzell's advice and branched out into other kinds of stories and articles in such publications as *American Mercury, The Christian Science Monitor,* and the University of California's *Western Folklore.*

Martha and I built a small but pleasant L-shaped house with redwood siding, a fireplace, and a big picture window. Our two daughters were born in the hospital just a block from our house, Melissa in 1950, Jennifer in 1952—two lovely redheads who brightened our days from the moments of their arrivals. It seemed that we were settling down to comfortable lives in an Oklahoma college town and that I was settling into a career as a teacher and writer.

And then, out of the blue, I had a chance to go to Africa as a Point Four technician. Oklahoma A.&M. had a contract with the Technical Cooperation Administration to help Ethiopia with its agricultural problems and to advise in the establishment of the country's first college of agriculture. Oklahoma A.&M. agricultural technicians had been going to Ethiopia for several years. Now the Ethiopian Ministry of Education wanted a team of Point Four workers to help in the creation of reading materials for the primary and secondary schools of the country. As an administrative convenience, the four educational technicians were to be recruited under the Oklahoma A.&M. contract. I was offered one of the jobs. The assignment would be for two years, and, of course, Martha and our daughters would go with me.

The decision to go to Ethiopia was easy to make. The opportunity to see some more of the world appealed as much to Martha as it did to me. Melissa was five and Jennifer three, both young enough to adjust easily to the change. I would be on leave from the English Department and would have a job to come back to. Always thinking about writing,

I envisioned the rich lode of story material that two years in Africa would yield. And although I don't remember thinking about all the foreign adventure books I had read as a boy, I'm sure they were there in my unconscious memory and that they were whispering to me, "Come on. Now's your chance. Don't pass it up."

In truth, the desire to be of service in a part of the world that needed help was probably the weakest of my several motives for wanting to go to Ethiopia. Yet it was a motive. I knew about the Marshall Plan's success. I had watched President Truman's skillful work with Congress in getting a foreign aid bill passed, and I was very much in favor of an international assistance program. I wanted to be a part of this new step in history that our country was taking.

Martha and I read as much about Ethiopia as we could and talked to A.&M. people who had been there. Located in the horn of Africa, Ethiopia is a country of towering mountains and what the eighteenth-century traveler James Bruce called "valleys of dreadful depth." Bruce had been searching for the source of the Blue Nile and found it in a vast lake, almost an inland sea, in the highlands of northwest Ethiopia. In ancient times, five hundred years before the birth of Christ, Ethiopia—known then as Aksum—was a powerful empire and, biblical scholars believe, perhaps the home of the Queen of Sheba.

But because of its isolation and rugged terrain, Ethiopia slipped from the pages of European history during the Middle Ages; one later historian wrote that it "wrapped itself in a cloak and slept for a thousand years." During the Crusades to recapture the Holy Land from the Arabs, Europeans began to hear rumors of a strange African kingdom ruled by a

Christian emperor called Prester John. English and French kings sent emissaries looking for Prester John, hoping he would help them in the fight for the Holy Land. They did not find Prester John, but in time Ethiopia was "rediscovered."

Except for a brief period of brutal Italian occupation beginning in 1936, Ethiopia had always been an independent country. With British help the Italian yoke was thrown off in 1941. Now Ethiopia, poor but proud, wanted to join the mainstream of the twentieth century and needed help to do so. The United States responded with the first big Point Four program in Africa.

In August, 1955, our Stillwater house leased for two years and our suitcases bulging, the Ashabranner family flew to Addis Ababa, the capital of Ethiopia. This was before the days of jet airplanes, and our flight was a long and tiring one; happily, Melissa and Jennifer proved to be great travelers, fascinated by every new thing they saw—and everything was new, except for a bagful of picture books we brought with us. The leg of the journey from New York to Rome took fifteen hours. We stopped in Rome for a day to stretch our legs, but we were so busy seeing things that we got little rest. The flight to Cairo was also long, and we had to wait in the airport from two A.M. until midmorning to catch our Ethiopian Airlines flight to Addis Ababa.

Curiously, my most vivid memory of the trip comes from a stop we made at a small desert airfield for refueling in the country of Sudan. While we watched from a scorchingly hot waiting room, a big tank of gasoline was hauled out to the plane on a cart pulled by two powerful water buffalo. In a

very real way that scene summed up for me the coming together at this point in history of the industrialized Western
world with the traditional world of Africa.

I had been assured by the Oklahoma A.&M. Ethiopian
contract office that we would be met at the airport in Addis
and that a house would be ready for us. It didn't happen
that way. When we arrived on a Sunday afternoon, no one
was there to meet us. The airport was small, crowded, noisy.
I found our bags—ten of them because we had an extra bag-
gage allowance—and put them in a big pile. Martha, Melissa,
and Jennifer sat on them while I wandered around, trying
to figure out what to do. I didn't know a word of Amharic,
the Ethiopian national language. I didn't have any Ethiopian
dollars, and at that time no facilities existed at the airport for
changing money. I had the names of a few people in the Point
Four office but no phone numbers and no coins to work the
public phone even if I had numbers. Martha and the girls
watched me from their perches on the bags and offered no
advice.

Finally, a consular officer from the American Embassy noticed my bewilderment and came to our rescue. He lent me
fifty Ethiopian dollars and suggested that I take my family
to the d'Itegue Hotel, the only hotel in Addis at that time
where foreigners stayed. He would take us, he said, but his
car was full with people he was meeting.

By the time we got our bags outside—even Jennifer dragged
one—all taxis were gone, but there were some gharries:
rubber-tired, horse-drawn carts with great red wheels and
bright, fringed awnings. I hired one, and, of course, Melissa
and Jennifer were delighted. No taxi could compete with a
gharry, and, in fact, it was a good way for us to have our
first look at Ethiopia: groves of beautiful tall and slender

eucalyptus trees, yellow flowers growing haphazardly every-where, small round huts with mud-coated walls and thatched roofs standing in the groves of trees, men and women wrapped in long white shawls called *shammas* walking along the narrow asphalt highway. Overhead the sky was a star-tling blue, but in the distance heavy rainy season clouds sat on top of a low mountain range. Ethiopia is near the equator, but the temperature that day of our arrival was wonderfully cool, as it is year round, we were to learn. The reason: Addis Ababa sits on a plateau at an elevation of over eight thousand feet.

Those were the good things we saw and felt on our gharry ride. As we entered Addis, we saw the other side: unbeliev-able squalor in slum sections of the city, open sewers or no sewers at all, children in rags, many of them sickly looking, beggars everywhere. Martha and I had read about this pov-erty; seeing it was another thing.

The d'Itegue Hotel was a big, dirty-brown stucco building with a tin roof. It had all the trappings of a first-class hotel—dining room, bar, lounge, barber service, a large staff—but there was a feeling of ancient shabbiness and uncleanliness about it. One thing was beautiful: a courtyard with radiant flower gardens.

Behind the hotel proper were several buildings of rooms; we stayed in one of those, in the only room left when we got to the hotel. It had two single beds, a table and two chairs. The floors were wooden and bare. There was a lavatory with taps marked *Chad* and *Frio*, hot and cold, but there was no hot water. Several health pamphlets we had been given had cautioned us not to drink water in Ethiopia unless we were sure it had been boiled; amoebic dysentery was only one of the disasters that might result from drinking tap water. I ordered a pot of hot tea, and we drank that and used it for brushing our teeth.

When we went to bed, the sheets were cold and damp, and the rainy season clouds had opened up. Martha and the girls went to sleep quickly, exhausted at the end of our journey. I lay awake for a long time, wondering just what I had got my family into.

# Point Four Assignment

**T**he next morning we began our new life. We awoke rested and refreshed; the cloudless sky overhead was again bright blue; the flower gardens in the courtyard sparkled; breakfast in the d'Itegue dining room was good. Even before we had finished eating, Bill Wrinkle, head of the Point Four education office showed up; the Embassy consular officer had called him about us. He apologized for the airport slip-up, although he was not to blame, and soon had us in a good temporary house.

In the next two whirlwind weeks, we got into our permanent house. Melissa began kindergarten at the American community school, which was run by Point Four wives who had managed to pool enough teaching credentials to satisfy U.S. State Department educational standards. The only nursery school in Addis was run by the small French community, and we enrolled Jennifer in it even though she didn't know a word of French. She soon made friends with a little French girl named Monique and sometimes went to her house after school. Before long Jennifer was showing off around home with words like *merci beaucoup* and *sil vous plait*. Martha was quickly absorbed in setting up our new home, learning to shop and bargain in the wonderful vegetable and spice market, and trying to find edible meat in the butcher's shop.

I met my Point Four colleagues in the educational materials development project: Russell Davis, an educational researcher with his doctorate from Harvard; Jim Chandler and Owen Loveless, both linguists from the University of Michigan. I also met the four bright young Ethiopians who were to work with us on the project: Hapte-ab Birou, Afewerk Mengesteb, Million Neqneq, and Amara Worku. The director general of the Ministry of Education emphasized to our Point Four team that he wanted us to teach our Ethiopian counterparts everything we could, not just do the work ourselves. We would be gone in a few years; they wouldn't.

The work was to produce reading materials, English learning materials, mathematics books, and other textbooks that were appropriate for Ethiopian elementary and high school students. Materials for the first four grades would all be in Amharic, for fifth grade up mostly in English because Ethiopia had made the decision that English would be the language of education.

At that time the only teaching and learning materials in the Ethiopian schools had been imported from overseas; almost nothing had been produced specifically for Ethiopian students. Education had almost disappeared under Italian occupation. The Ministry of Education had done a heroic job of getting schools started again in the ten years since the Italians were driven out, but still there was almost everything to do. Not more than 10 percent of school-age children were in schools, and the national illiteracy rate was over 90 percent. The schools in Addis were fairly well supplied with books, but the situation in hinterland schools was desperate.

I sat in on an English class in a remote town in Shoa Province where all the teacher had to teach with was half a dozen copies of *The Vicar of Wakefield* by Oliver Goldsmith, the eighteenth-century Anglo-Irish writer. I can't imagine where the books came from, probably the gift of a British publisher. I had read *The Vicar of Wakefield* in a graduate course on the English novel and had found it hard going. I wondered what these young Ethiopians were getting out of it. They said, quite sensibly, that they were learning English words from it.

Bill Wrinkle told me that my job was to get something to read into the hands of primary- and middle-grade students, both in Amharic and English, and to get it to them fast. He didn't care what it was as long as the students could understand it and learn something about Ethiopia from it. The director general agreed with Bill. I told them that was fine; I would do it but that I had to learn something about Ethiopia first. Russ Davis was going to work on a series of math books and readers in Amharic, and he felt the same way I did about getting to know the people and their country. Russ was a gifted language learner; by the time he had been in Addis a few weeks, he was speaking Amharic, as well as writing it. I struggled with the language the whole time I was in Ethiopia; I never got really good with it, but I never gave up.

Soon Russ and I and Owen Loveless—who was even more absorbed in Amharic than Russ—and two of our counterparts, Amara and Million, set out on an educational safari that took us from Addis Ababa to the northern edge of Ethiopia and back again in a month's time. We traveled by Land Rover, slept under the stars, sometimes on the floor of a schoolhouse, and occasionally in a hotel bed. The roads were sometimes fairly good, sometimes tracks we could barely see. We climbed towering mountains and descended into the "valleys of dreadful depth." We crossed the Tigre plain, which seemed endless, and finally reached the shores of the Red Sea, where the heat was withering.

We talked to headmasters, teachers, and students in every town we passed through; the message from teachers was always the same: send us teaching and learning materials. We talked to farmers, village leaders, and old men and women who told us stories they had learned from their grandparents. A few years later Russ and I wrote an article for *The Horn Book Magazine* about some of our experiences on that first trip through Ethiopia. Here is the way the article began:

*Haik* is a lovely lake high in the mountains of central Ethiopia. *Haik* is actually the Amharic word for lake, but so important is this body of water to the people living around it that it has no other name. It is simply *Haik,* the lake. It gives the lake dwellers abundant fish; it gives them water; it gives them reeds for mats and for their curious little boats; on a small island at its center, it shelters the ancient and revered monastery of St. Stephen's.

We were on our way to Aksum, holy city of Ethiopia, and had stopped to make night camp at the edge of *Haik.* As we unloaded our Land Rover, an old monk from St. Stephen's wandered by and stopped to watch us. We talked to him, and he told us that he was a bird watcher in a monastery cornfield nearby. All day long he sat on a little elevated platform in the center of the field and threw rocks to frighten away the marauding birds.

"It is a job for children or very old men," he said. "The child will do the job because he becomes interested in it. The old man will do the job because he has patience."

"But it is an important job," we said.

"Oh, yes," he agreed, "it is important. Without the watcher, birds would grow fat and men would starve. God is good to give old men such important work."

"Have you been many years at the monastery?" we asked him.

"Since I was a boy of eight," the old monk replied. "I was here even before Menelik defeated our enemies at Aduwa."

Here seemed to be just the man we were looking for: one old enough in the area to know its oral traditions, clear-minded enough to remember details, possessed of a certain facility with words, and holding a clear set of beliefs and values. Such a combination often returns rich dividends for the folklorist.

Our man was as good as he promised to be. We drew him out slowly; and as shadows lengthened beside our Land Rover, he told us story after story that he had heard since his boyhood. Once he was warmed up, he felt no shyness about talking into the microphone of our battery-run tape recorder. In fact, after he heard his own voice on our playback, he seemed to enjoy himself immensely.

Inevitably many of his stories dealt with the lake that was so important to the life of the region. He told us of the wicked people who had once made human sacrifices to a huge water serpent which they believed to be the spirit of the lake. He told us of a great holy man who came into the land and was outraged at the wickedness of the lake people. The holy man set the waters of the lake afire to show the people the power of the true God, and from that day they were all Christians and the monastery of St. Stephen's was founded. The old monk told us how the clever monkey had tricked all the other animals into thinking that the lake water was poison so that he could have it all to himself. He not only knew folk stories, but had given some thought to the whys and wherefores of the tales. He said: "The tale must teach something important or I, an old man, would not bother to squat among noisy children to tell them stories. And then the tale must entertain, or children would not bother to squat down to listen to a dull, old man.''

Later, as we sat around our campfire, the vividness of the old bird watcher's tales lingered on and sharpened our awareness of the sights and sounds around us—the night cries of unseen animals, the moonlight floating like a golden film on the lake, the dark, crouching bulk of the encircling mountains. The stories became sharp, were more enjoyable for us because we had heard them in their own setting and from the mouth of a man who had known them from childhood.

When we returned to Addis, I knew infinitely more about Ethiopia than I had known, and just as important, I knew how very much more I had to learn. But now it was time to put some real Ethiopian reading material into the hands of Ethiopian school students. I went back into my boyhood reading memories and came out with the idea that we should produce the Ethiopian equivalent of *My Weekly Reader* and *Junior Scholastic.* That is what we did, publishing a simple four-page fold-over in Amharic for the primary grades and a twelve-page magazine in English for the middle grades. The middle-grade magazine was called *Time to Read* and the primary-grade leaflet *Yemambeb Gize,* which in Amharic also means "time to read."

Both magazines contained folktales, history, and current events—all Ethiopian. We used jokes and riddles and sometimes ran easy-to-understand articles on health, nutrition, and other practical subjects. We published both *Yemambeb Gize* and *Time to Read* every month of the school year; the printing was done on the press in the Point Four audiovisual center, which also was used as a training facility for Ethiopians. The print order for *Yemambeb Gize* was twenty-five thousand, for *Time to Read,* ten thousand. Those numbers couldn't begin to cover all Ethiopian schools, but it was a start. After a few trial issues, the cost of publishing the magazines was built into the Ministry of Education budget. We got the magazines out to the schools by any means we could: trucks, buses, Ethiopian Airlines, Land Rovers carrying ministry people around the country.

I'm sure our magazines would not have won any literary prizes, but I am certain that they filled a desperate need in Ethiopian schools of that time. I was in provincial schools several times when *Yemambeb Gize* or *Time to Read* arrived. One of the warmest memories I have from my years of working overseas is seeing Ethiopian students receiving their copy of one of the magazines. That moment was always "time to read," and that is what the students did, quietly and with complete absorption. A few days later, after they had been over everything with the teacher, they would take their copy home. More than once I saw a student reading to his parents or grandparents.

Martha became involved in Ethiopian education in a very special way. Empress Menen School, a good school for girls in Addis, needed a home economics teacher, and the principal learned about Martha's background in that field. She was asked to teach sewing (machine), cooking, and nutrition to upper level girls. Martha had never taught, even practice teaching, and she fretted about whether she could do it. But she took the assignment, and I heard from many Empress Menen teachers that she did a fine job. I know that she often spent hours the night before the next day's class getting her teaching materials ready.

Martha's most vivid memory of teaching at Empress Menen is what she calls the "cookie caper." In 1956 the school, which was founded in 1931 by Ethiopia's Empress Menen, decided to have a silver anniversary celebration. Both Emperor Haile Selassie and the Empress agreed to attend. Martha and her cooking class were asked to make cookies, and make them they did, over a thousand, using some of Martha's favorite recipes for brownies, oatmeal cookies, almond cookies, and others.

The day before the celebration word came that the royal couple would have to postpone their visit for two weeks. The staff and students of Empress Menen School ate the thousand cookies rather than let them grow stale; then Martha and her girls had to bake another thousand fresh ones. This time the Emperor and Empress and many other dignitaries came, and the cookies were a great success.

Martha, Melissa, and Jennifer traveled with me in the provinces a number of times. Everything was discovery and adventure. Our Land Rover got stuck in deep mud at Lake Awasa one evening, about 150 miles from Addis Ababa. Everything I tried to get it unstuck just made the rear wheels dig in deeper. We had no camping gear with us; I built a big fire, and Martha and I sat up all night keeping it going while Melissa and Jennifer slept in the Land Rover. Just before dark, we caught a glimpse of a leopard in the trees, and all night we listened to the cries of animals and the calls of night birds. The next morning a group of strong young Ethiopian men came along and pushed the Land Rover out of the mud. I gave each one an Ethiopian dollar, about forty cents in American money, and they were amazed at my generosity.

We saw the wild animals of Ethiopia: hyenas, Grant's gazelle, ostriches (in the Rift Valley), wild goats, tiny antelope called dik-dik, and many more. Once we were with a game officer when a troop of baboons crossed the road. He told us to watch carefully, and he described what we were seeing. First, baboon scouts came to look over the place where the troop would cross. Then the big soldier baboons stationed themselves on each side of the road. Only then did the young baboons, the females, and the old ones scurry across the road.

"With such organization and discipline," the game officer said, "is it any wonder our farmers have such a hard time keeping baboons from stealing their crops?"

Everywhere we went, we made friends with Ethiopia and Ethiopians.

Suddenly two years had passed, and the time to leave had come. I couldn't believe how swiftly the months had flown; I felt that I was still settling in and learning my work. The chairman of the Oklahoma A.&M. English Department wrote that I was expected back. He said I would be promoted from instructor to assistant professor.

But we never got back to Oklahoma except for short visits. The Technical Cooperation Administration in Washington wanted me to join that organization and go to the North African country of Libya, to do the same kind of educational materials development I had done in Ethiopia. Martha and I knew that we had come to a major fork in the road of our life. I had read Robert Frost's poetry since I was a boy. During those weeks of decision, I remember thinking many times about his lovely poem, "The Road Not Taken."

We decided that we wanted to go on living and working in developing countries. I was sure I wanted to do more of what I had been doing in Ethiopia. We went to Libya for two years and then transferred to the West African nation of Nigeria. The experiences were always different: new people to meet and work with, new customs to learn, new foods to eat, new languages to struggle with. My work was sometimes frustrating, sometimes discouraging, often wonderfully rewarding. Never did Martha or I regret the decision we had made.

Of course, we thought about Melissa and Jennifer. We thought about them all the time. We knew they were missing valuable experiences by not growing up and going to school in their own country. Fortunately, the quality of the schools they went to overseas was not a problem. In Libya they attended an American school at Wheelus Air Force Base near Tripoli; in Lagos, Nigeria, they went to a small private British school that took the fundamentals of reading, writing, and mathematics very seriously.

What Melissa and Jennifer were missing by not growing up in the United States we felt was being offset by a wealth of experiences in the countries in which we lived. They were meeting new people, absorbing new cultures, discovering new ways of looking at the world. For example, I had grown up in Oklahoma without getting to know a single black person except for my brother's sparring partner, Vernon. Melissa's best friend in Nigeria was a black American girl, Marcia Johnson, the daughter of a colleague of mine in the foreign aid program. Jennifer's best friend, Marguerite Ware, was also the daughter of a black American foreign aid worker. When the Wares were transferred to the Northern Nigeria city of Kano, Jennifer made her first plane trip by herself to visit Marguerite for a week.

Living and working overseas changed my writing completely. There was nothing unusual about that; I had new experiences and new material to write about. What I didn't expect was that I also would change my audience. In past years I had written only for adults, but now I felt that what I was learning about other cultures and about people of different cultures understanding each other would be interesting to young readers. After we left Ethiopia, Russ Davis and I wrote some books together, even though he was in America and we seldom saw each other face to face. We wrote a book of Ethiopian folktales called *The Lion's Whiskers* and a book of stories about Point Four workers. We wrote two books about West Africa.

When I was a boy, I had wanted to write stories about strange people in faraway place. Now I was writing stories like that, but the people didn't seem strange, and the places didn't seem faraway.

# The Peace Corps Is Born

**O**n the night of October 13, 1960, in New York, Senator John F. Kennedy engaged Richard Nixon, his rival for the Presidency of the United States, in the third of their nationally televised debates. Immediately after the debate, Kennedy and his staff rushed to LaGuardia Airport and flew to Willow Run Airport, an hour's drive from the University of Michigan, where Kennedy was scheduled to speak briefly. It was almost two A.M. when the Kennedy party arrived at the university. Some of his staff had advised canceling the engagement, fearing hardly anyone would be waiting at such a late hour, but Kennedy had insisted on going.

The night was clear and mild, and to the campaign party's astonishment a huge turnout of students, estimated at ten thousand, had waited up for the senator. Making his way to the Student Union Building and standing on the steps there, Kennedy spoke without notes and put his thoughts in the form of questions to the students. He asked how many of them would be willing to give up a part of their lives to work in Africa, Asia, and Latin America for the good of the people in those places and as a service to the United States. He asked whether they would contribute two years or more to the betterment of the poor countries of the world.

In 1960 the cold war with Russia was a bitter reality, and U.S. competition with the Communist giant was clearly on Kennedy's mind when he said, ". . . on your willingness to contribute part of your life to this country, I think, will depend the answer whether we as a free society can compete."

Less than a month later, on November 2, in a major address at the Cow Palace in San Francisco, Kennedy put on record his intention to create a Peace Corps if he were elected President. Speaking of the need for greater American effort in the developing countries of Africa, Asia, and Latin America, Kennedy said, "I therefore propose that our inadequate efforts in this area be supplemented by a Peace Corps of talented young men and women, willing and able to serve their country. . . ." This was Kennedy's first public use of the term "Peace Corps."

The Peace Corps had now become a Kennedy campaign pledge and thus a campaign issue. Richard Nixon attacked the idea, saying a Peace Corps would be "a haven for draft dodgers." He also said that the idea was "superficial" and had been "conceived solely for campaign purposes."

But Nixon was wrong. John F. Kennedy won the election and created the Peace Corps by executive order on March 1, 1961, less than six weeks after he took the oath of office as President. It was his first major act as President, and the speed with which he moved made clear the importance he attached to the Peace Corps.

Kennedy appointed his brother-in-law Robert Sargent Shriver to be head of the Peace Corps and challenged the new organization "to be in business by Monday morning." It was. After the Peace Corps had become a huge success,

Shriver liked to joke that the President had made him director because it would be easier to fire a relative in case the Peace Corps fell on its face. But Sarge, as everyone called him, had no intention of letting that happen. A dynamic and tireless leader, he quickly put together a headquarters staff and hammered out the guidelines for the new organization:

The Peace Corps would be made up of volunteers who would receive no salary, only a modest living allowance.

Volunteers would be well qualified for the work they were sent to do.

They would live among the people they were sent to help, in villages or wherever else it might be, with no special housing or other privileges.

They would serve for two years, a period that could be extended if everyone agreed.

With these principles in place, Shriver set out around the world to see what countries would be interested in receiving Peace Corps volunteers. One of his first stops was the West African country of Nigeria; with over 40 million people, Nigeria was Africa's most populous nation. It had won its independence from Great Britain only the year before, in 1960, and was sure to become one of the leaders of the African continent.

I was working for the United States Agency for International Development (USAID) in Lagos, Nigeria, when Shriver flew in. I had followed the birth of the Peace Corps with great interest and was excited by the idea. I certainly had nothing against our foreign aid program, but I thought that the addition of thousands of young Americans working in Africa, Asia, and Latin America—working in the villages and rural towns, living with the people—could add an important dimension to the U.S. effort to help poor countries.

I felt that if the Peace Corps could keep going long enough to put a hundred thousand young American men and women overseas and keep them there in productive work for two years, the countries they served in were sure to benefit. I was positive that America would benefit from what these young people would learn about developing countries and from what they would learn about themselves.

Since the Peace Corps as yet had no staff in Nigeria—or any other country—USAID was asked to arrange Shriver's schedule. I volunteered for the assignment, and everyone in USAID and the American Embassy was happy to let me do the job. Although the Peace Corps idea was exciting, no one was at all certain how it was going to work out in practice. Many American ambassadors were privately horrified at the prospect of hundreds of soft, young Americans scattered throughout the countries they were responsible for. One critic called the Peace Corps "the most dangerous experiment since the children's crusade."

Shriver and members of his Washington staff arrived in Nigeria on April 25, less than two months after the Peace Corps had come into existence. If they had any doubts about the new organization, those doubts didn't show. Shriver had already rejected advice that the Peace Corps begin slowly with small pilot projects. He knew what the President wanted: a fast start and programs big enough to make a difference. Sarge was determined to give the President what he wanted.

Shriver was warmly received by all Nigerian government officials; everyone knew that the Peace Corps was a program close to President Kennedy's heart. Shriver met with Prime Minister Sir Abubakar Tafawa Balewa, who warmly endorsed the Peace Corps idea. Shriver then visited the three regional capitals of Nigeria and explained the Peace Corps to the regional leaders.

In contrast to USAID and United Nations technical assistance programs, Shriver said, Peace Corps volunteers would not be advisors or expert consultants but rather "doers," persons who would do jobs as teachers, surveyors, engineers, or in whatever field jobs needed doing. They would work side by side with Nigerians. I went with Shriver on all of his visits to the regions, and I could see that his explanation of what volunteers would do appealed to officials everywhere.

Although I did not officially join the Peace Corps staff until mid-August, I never worked another day for USAID after Shriver's visit to Nigeria. It just seemed to be assumed that I would carry on the Peace Corps' business after Shriver and his team left, and I did.

But Shriver was completely candid with me. He told me that he wanted me to set up the Nigeria program and run it as acting Peace Corps director until he could find an outstanding black American educator to be the number one person; at that point I would become the deputy director. Shriver felt strongly that the most populous black nation in Africa should have a black Peace Corps director who would have the stature, as he put it, "to almost be a second ambassador."

I understood Shriver's point of view and accepted on the terms he outlined. I told him, though, that if all went well, I would someday like to run a Peace Corps program without the "acting" in front of my title. Shriver said he understood, but he made no promise.

The three regions poured in requests for more than twelve hundred volunteers; they asked for over fifty different kinds of professional workers, everything from teachers to architects, soil analysts, mechanical engineers, and cost accountants. They even wanted two boat builders and three rubber technologists! But the central government in Lagos decided to limit the number of volunteers the first year to 25 percent of the total requests; they also decided that the first volunteers to come to Nigeria should all be classroom teachers, mostly in secondary schools.

Washington was quite relieved at both of these restrictions. In the United States thousands of people were applying for service in the Peace Corps, but 90 percent of those who applied were young men and women just graduated from college. That was fine, but there weren't many boat builders and irrigation specialists among them. The selection division in Washington was working around the clock to select the best qualified applicants—not only for Nigeria but for a number of other countries—and get them into training programs.

Harvard and the University of California at Los Angeles (UCLA) agreed to train the first groups of volunteers for Nigeria. There was no way that three months of training in teaching methods, no matter how intensive, could make experienced teachers out of recent college graduates, but it would give them a start; selection would ensure that they had excellent academic records in their subjects. Beyond that, we were convinced that the enthusiasm and dedication they would bring to their work would make them valuable teachers in the Nigerian schools. Fortunately, instruction in the Nigerian secondary schools was in English.

While the volunteers were in training, one of my biggest jobs was to visit the schools where they were going to teach. I had to make sure there was a real need for a Peace Corps teacher, that the headmaster knew the volunteer was coming, and that he or she had a place to live. I can't remember the number of times the house the volunteer was to occupy proved to be a foundation or a marked-off plot plus a thoroughly well-intentioned assurance by the headmaster that the house would be finished by the time the volunteer arrived. I can't remember the number of times I received letters from volunteers, once they had arrived at their schools, asking me how I expected them to live in a foundation. But they always found some way to make do.

Nigeria is more than twice the size of California, and the roads are long and rough and dusty. I pounded through the country for two months, and the best I could do was a very superficial job of checking schools. Whenever friends could take care of Melissa and Jennifer, Martha came with me to help take notes. A site survey visit usually amounted to arriving in a cloudburst of dust, having a cup of tea with the headmaster, walking through the school, and looking at the volunteer's prospective house. Then it was on to the next location, a drive of from four hours to a whole day. Sometimes, of course, there was an overnight, and these were good for longer talks and a better feel for the realities of teaching in Nigeria.

Despite their desperate need for teachers, not every education official in the regions was eager to get Peace Corps volunteers that first year. Hector Jelf, a tough, plain-talking Englishman who had been permanent secretary of the Ministry of Education in Northern Nigeria for many years, told me quite bluntly at our first meeting that he would prefer to wait a year and see how the volunteers did in the other two regions of Nigeria. Jelf told me that the care and feeding of foreign teachers had always been one of his biggest headaches and that he had had particular trouble with the few American teachers he had been able to recruit.

"They have no idea what it's like to live and teach in an African school," he said. "I hired five last year and four of

them were gone before the second term was well under-
way."

Jelf finally asked for some volunteers but chiefly because
his Minister of Education didn't want the Northern Region
to be the only one left out of the new Peace Corps thing.

And then the volunteers began to arrive in Lagos from their
training programs, planeloads of them. With everyone of
those first groups I had the same reactions. One was how
young they looked. The other was how keenly they wanted
to be good Peace Corps volunteers. It is true that they had
many motives for joining the Peace Corps: a yearning for
adventure, postponing a career decision, a desire for a change
from college before going on to graduate school. Some simply
wanted to take a look at the world; a few sought to delay
military service (although that was not often a motive until
the mid-sixties when the war in Vietnam became a bitter and
divisive national issue).

But in almost every case an additional motive was present:
they wanted to make a contribution to a better world in a
personal, individual way. A great many of the early volunteers had a deep feeling for President Kennedy, and they
believed they were answering his call to national duty in a
new and constructive way that he had made possible. They
took very seriously what he had said about building a better
America through helping the poor countries of the world.

Speaking of Kennedy, one of the first volunteers said, "He
made being an American exciting."

After a few days of orientation in Lagos, the newly arrived
group of volunteers would go their different ways to their
schools. Most would travel by bus but some by train or plane;
a telegram was always sent to the headmaster telling him

when his volunteer would arrive, but we could never be sure that the message would be delivered in remote areas. Sometimes a headmaster came to Lagos to collect "his" volunteer and take him to the school. Everyone liked that arrangement. The headmaster had a chance to come to the big city, and the trip back provided a chance to get acquainted.

The first few days at the school were interesting, even exciting, as the volunteer met his headmaster, was assigned his classes, became acquainted with his fellow teachers, and went to town to buy food and some things for his house. Getting to town was a problem because secondary schools in the regions were usually located several miles outside the nearest town, and sometimes they were much more isolated than that. Since the volunteer didn't have a car, he had to wait for a bus that might pass by the school once a day or get a ride with the headmaster, usually the only person at the school who had a vehicle.

The volunteer knew that there were differences between African schools, which were based on the British system, and schools in America in which he had grown up. When his classes started, he learned just how great the differences were. Each course had a detailed syllabus or summary covering everything the student was expected to know in order to pass a test that would be given by national examiners at the end of school. Whether the student received his school-leaving certificate and thus became eligible for university entrance or for employment with the government depended entirely on whether he passed the national examination with a good mark. The good teacher, therefore, was the one who covered the syllabus material most carefully and closely and coached his students to parrot back answers to the syllabus questions. Whether they understood what the answers meant made no difference.

84

In Northern Nigeria, 1961. An African folktale says that an angry giant pulled the baobab tree out of the ground and stuck it back upside down. Since then the roots have been where the branches should be.

Jackie Kennedy meets a group of Peace Corps volunteers in New Delhi, 1962.

Pondering a Persian wheel, a primitive irrigation method, at a farm in the Punjab, India, 1963.

With Jack Vaughn, director of the Peace Corps, on Vaughn's first trip to India, 1965. Photograph by R.N. Khanna.

The Ashabranner family in New Delhi, 1963. In the background is one of
the ancient Lodi Tombs.

Being sworn in as deputy director of the Peace Corps by Vice President
Hubert Humphrey, 1967. Peace Corps director, Jack Vaughn, looks on.

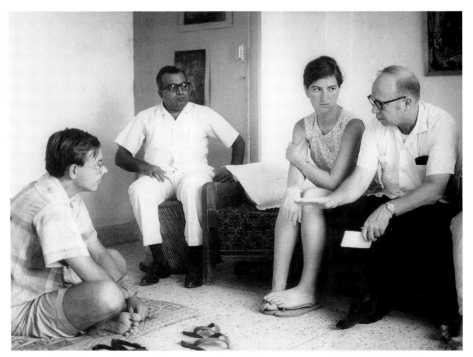

With Peace Corps volunteers and an Indian government official, Punjab,
India, 1969.

Melissa with her proud parents on
her graduation day from Yale, 1980.

Jennifer at her high school
graduation, Kensington,
Maryland, 1971.

Melissa and her father today.

Jennifer with her father,
Williamsburg, Virginia.

Giancarlo

At the Vietnam Veterans Memorial with a group of fifth and sixth grade students from Sheldon Elementary School, Sheldon, Vermont. One of the books they read in preparation for their trip to Washington, D.C., was *Always to Remember*. Photograph by Jennifer Ashabranner.

Brent Ashabranner today.

Teaching like this was no fun, the volunteer quickly decided. Where were the young minds he was supposed to open up? In addition, the volunteer was having a very rough time with loneliness and homesickness. He was practically trapped in the hot, dusty, treeless school compound. Even if he had had a car, there was nothing in the nearby town to attract him but more heat and dust, a few stores, and a vegetable market.

The volunteer missed the other volunteers he had gone through training with, and he missed the life he had left in the States. Sometimes at night before going to sleep he could actually smell a steak cooking on a charcoal grill. He could hear the faint hum of the air conditioner in his room at home and feel the soft coolness. He would think about the girl he had dated during his senior year, and he remembered the car he had passed on to his younger brother. He wondered how the Dallas Cowboys were doing.

On my first round of visits to the volunteers after they had gone to their teaching assignments, I found the conditions I have just described almost everywhere. One volunteer in a particularly isolated school was half dead with loneliness and homesickness. We talked almost all night, and every half hour or so he would say, "I'm not going to be the first one to quit."

He didn't quit at all, and neither did any of the other volunteers in those first groups that came to Nigeria. They were volunteers, and the Peace Corps would have bought anyone a ticket home if he—or she—said he couldn't make it. But no one said that.

And slowly, as the volunteer stayed longer at the school, the situation began to change. He developed a special relationship with a few of his students, who seemed to know why he wanted to go beyond the syllabus. Sometimes they came to his house at night and talked. They talked about the subject he was teaching and about other things. They had many questions about America, and he had many about Nigeria. They learned from each other. And he formed real friendships with one or two of the Nigerian teachers.

One of the best times came on a holiday when one of his students asked him to come home with him. They traveled by lorry to a village about a hundred miles from the school, and there the volunteer felt that he was finally in the "real" Africa. He met his student's parents, slept in their hut, watched the holiday dances, and ate the chicken with fiery sauce that had been prepared especially for him. He tried out his halting Yoruba or Hausa or Ibo and was pleased that he could understand a little bit of what people said to him.

And at the school, as he won the confidence of the headmaster and the other teachers, the volunteer discovered that he could do some things that were closer to what he had originally expected to do. He got the tiny library in better shape, organized a science or drama club, cleaned up the chemistry lab, tutored students who needed special help, and gave help in English no matter what his subject was. Little by little in the classroom he got beyond the syllabus with some new ideas.

The most incredible episode in all my years in the Peace Corps involved a volunteer teacher. One morning I received a frantic phone call in my Lagos office. The caller shouted that the volunteer teacher assigned to a school near the city had been bitten by a green mamba, an extremely venomous West African snake. I rushed to the school and found the volunteer waiting at the roadside with two of his students and the dead snake.

As we drove to the hospital, I got the story. The volunteer, who was wearing shorts, had gone to his house between classes and just as he entered had been struck on the leg by the snake. The volunteer ran to the kitchen, picked up a butcher knife, and killed the snake. He then took his snakebite kit, which we issued to all volunteers, and walked to his next class. He told his students what had happened and then said, "If you ever get bitten by a poisonous snake this is what you should do."

He proceeded to take the razor blade from the snakebite kit, cut the proper cross over the wound made by the snake's fangs, and draw out the blood with the suction cup. He explained that if the victim did not have that kind of equipment, he could suck out the blood and spit it out, or have someone else do it for him. The students told me this story in awe, and I am sure I looked awestruck as well.

At the hospital the snake was positively identified as a green mamba, and the volunteer was given an injection of antivenin. He had some reaction either to the snake's poison that still remained in his system or to the horse serum in the antivenin but he soon recovered with no ill effects.

Many volunteers over the years found that they could introduce more imaginative teaching methods into a classroom dominated by lectures and dictation of notes. I don't believe, however, that anyone ever used the show-and-tell method quite as dramatically as the snakebitten volunteer from the school near Lagos.

I was proud of the Peace Corps volunteer teachers I knew and worked with in Nigeria. They were pioneers in a very real way, tackling tough assignments and finding ways to do what the Peace Corps expected of them. The good Peace Corps volunteer teacher—and most were good—knew his subject and taught it well. But he made just as important a contribution by giving his students the example of a teacher who had a human concern for the well-being of his students, who took an interest in them as individuals, and who considered that their problems were important and worth listening to.

Tai Solarin, a Nigerian headmaster and highly regarded newspaper columnist who had watched the Peace Corps teachers in action for some time, wrote in one of his articles: "I believe in my heart of hearts that a lubrication of our teaching force with the Peace Corps is a greater service to this country than Britain did in a hundred years with all the epauletted and sword-carrying Governors who ever ruled this country."

After the first term in 1962, I saw Hector Jelf, the Northern Region permanent secretary who had taken Peace Corps teachers with the greatest reluctance because he thought they would resign and go home when they found out what teaching in an African school was like.

"I won't say your Peace Corps volunteers are the greatest teachers I ever saw," Jelf said gruffly, "but I will say they stay on the job."

His roster showed that not one volunteer had resigned from his post during that term, and his roster was quite correct.

At the height of the Peace Corps program in Nigeria—long after I had left—550 volunteer teachers were in classroom assignments. At that time, a high-ranking officer in the Ministry of Education expressed his feelings quite clearly. "There is," he said, "not one of the various foreign aid schemes working in this country that can beat the Peace Corps."

In early 1962, Shriver found the black educator he wanted to be director of the Peace Corps program in Nigeria. He was Dr. Samuel Proctor, President of North Carolina Agricultural and Technical College. Dynamic, wise, a good manager, Sam Proctor took over the reins of the program, and I became his deputy. We worked well together from the beginning, and I was pleased, when I left Nigeria in July, that Ambassador Joseph Palmer wrote Shriver a letter saying that Sam and I were "a fine team, if I ever saw one."

With our two years in Nigeria at an end, Martha and I decided the time had come for our family to return to the United States for a while. We had lived in various parts of Africa for seven years, and we thought that my working for the Peace Corps in Washington for a year or so would give us a chance to get our roots back into native soil. Bill Moyers, who was on Shriver's personal staff and soon would become deputy director of the Peace Corps, told me there were a number of useful jobs I could do in Washington.

When we reached Washington in September, I found the staff there in a lather of activity because 1962 had become a year of unrestrained growth for the Peace Corps. By the end of 1961 volunteers were in nine countries. In 1962 programs were developed in twenty-eight new countries and volunteers recruited to fill them. Most volunteers continued to be classroom teachers, but other kinds of programs were developing. In some countries volunteers were working in community development, agriculture, road surveying, and as engineers, nurses, and mechanics.

I had been in Washington but a few days when Shriver called me in. He started talking about India and its importance and how he felt the Peace Corps might do some of its best work there. I wondered if Sarge had got me mixed up with someone else. Then he told me that he had finally found the man he wanted to be the first Peace Corps director in India. The man was Charles Houston. He was a medical doctor; he had done pioneer work on the development of a mechanical heart; he was a well-known mountain climber who had been in the assault party on the mighty Himalayan peak

89

K-2. Houston had written a stirring account of the climb in his book, *K-2: The Savage Mountain.*

Sarge's eyes glowed as he described what was obviously his vision of the perfect Peace Corps director for a major country: a man of proven professional ability, a man with a questing scientific mind, a man of adventurous spirit, an articulate man. "But he doesn't know item one about administration or working with foreign governments," Shriver said. "That's why I want you to go to India with him and be his deputy."

I tried to tell Sarge about our plans to buy a house in Washington and get to know the country again, but he kept talking about India, the possibilities for the Peace Corps there, the interest that the great Indian leader Jawaharlal Nehru had in the Peace Corps idea.

As many men and women found out in those years, saying no to Sargent Shriver was almost impossible. Half an hour after I left his office I called Martha and told her that Shriver wanted us to go to India. She was silent a moment and then said, "I haven't unpacked. If you want to go, I'm ready."

And so it was decided. Melissa and Jennifer, overseas veterans now, also were ready to go. We learned that there was a good international school in New Delhi, where we would live. We were in India for four years; the first two, I was Charlie Houston's deputy; the last two I was the director of the Peace Corps program. They were good years for all of us.

# *My Peace Corps*

**M**y years with the Peace Corps spanned all of President Kennedy's tragically short administration, all of President Johnson's, and the early months of President Nixon's. During those eight and a half years, I saw the Peace Corps grow from an idea in a campaign speech to an organization with more than 15,000 volunteers working in sixty countries around the world. Over 35,000 volunteers and staff served in the Peace Corps during the time I was in it, and I knew many hundreds of them personally.

Almost all of those I knew well built up a tremendous emotional investment in their Peace Corps service. The source of that investment for volunteers was two years or more of the closest association with people—often the most desperately poor and wretchedly underprivileged people of the earth—under conditions that were frustrating, rewarding, delicate, and strange. The concerns, the loyalties, the affections that developed had a powerful emotional base. The experiences were intensely personal; in a sense there were almost as many Peace Corps as there were Peace Corps volunteers and staff.

The experiences of a Peace Corps staff person were, of course, quite different from those of volunteers. He spent his time working with government officials in developing new programs and in trying, with varying degrees of success, to help volunteers in their work. Between those two jobs, the staff person probably built an emotional investment in the Peace Corps that, while different, was equal to that of the volunteer.

My own personal Peace Corps contains such memories as that of the volunteer in Nigeria bitten by the green mamba and the drowning in the Bay of Bengal of one of the loveliest women volunteers I ever knew. I remember worrying day and night about our volunteers working in the Punjab during the India-Pakistan conflict of 1965 and my difficult decision (when I was briefly acting director of the Peace Corps in Washington) to remove our volunteers from the Eastern Region of Nigeria during the tragic civil war of 1967.

There are very different kinds of memories. I remember at the end of a frustrating day of desk work in New Delhi picking up a letter from a schoolgirl in the south Indian city of Visakhapatnam, where we had a volunteer teacher assigned. The letter contained a poem entitled, "Thank You, America, for Sending Margery Donk." The meter in the poem was rather shaky, and the girl's heroic efforts to find words that rhymed with "Donk" were not very successful. But there was no questioning the depth of feeling the girl had for her Peace Corps volunteer teacher.

Margery changed her name to Mrs. Richard Beeler when she married a volunteer who was teaching in a nearby town. They came to New Delhi for the wedding, and I stood in for

Margery's father when the moment came to give her away. I'm not sure I can remember all the Peace Corps brides I gave away, but they are part of my emotional investment in the Peace Corps. So were the several godchildren that Martha and I acquired during the Peace Corps years.

Memories from our years in India are rich beyond measure.

Larry Tecker was a brash young volunteer in the Punjab. He had never given a thought to college, but he was a good heavy equipment mechanic, and he trained Indian mechanics in the public works department. He was high-spirited and headstrong, and I had doubts about whether he would get through two years in India. Not only did he get through, he won a special commendation from the public works department. When he returned to the United States, Larry decided to go to college. He became a lawyer, worked as a public defender for several years, then became one of the top lawyers on the American island of Guam in the Pacific. He and his lovely family live there today. Perhaps the Peace Corps did not redirect Larry Tecker's life, but I'm sure it helped.

Logan Sallada was a volunteer working in a remote town near India's border with China and the ancient country of Tibet that had been taken over by the Chinese. In 1963 the Dalai Lama—the spiritual leader of Tibet—and thousands of his people fled to India to escape Chinese persecution. They set up their wretched refugee camps near the town where Logan worked. He made friends with the refugees and made frequent trips to New Delhi, pounding on international agency doors until the refugees began to receive medical and other supplies. Logan helped to set up a marketing outlet for Tibetan refugee rugs and handicrafts in New Delhi and even in the United States. He became a legend among the Tibetan refugees and extended his time as a Peace Corp volunteer for a year so that he could continue to help them. Logan's was the kind of story that Kipling could have told wonderfully.

I once visited a volunteer named Martin Ross who lived in a small village where he was doing farm extension work; he also had a demonstration plot where at the time he was raising sweet potatoes. I remember very clearly that we had a lunch of sweet, hot tea and bananas and then walked three miles in the midday heat across the fields to look at his demonstration crop.

Marty was pleased with his sweet potatoes, which he said were ready for harvesting and would really impress the local farmers. He dug down in the ground to show me a specimen. There was nothing there. He dug in another spot and came up empty-handed. He tried again and again with the same result. Someone had stolen every potato and carefully replaced the vines over the ground.

Marty stood there a moment, thoughtfully, with his head down. "Well," he said, "everyone in this village is hungry." As we walked back to his one-room house, he managed a smile and said, "Anyway, the word will get around about how big and sweet those potatoes are, and that's why I raised them."

Volunteers like Marty had a dogged determination. He planted another demonstration crop as soon as he could.

Two farm extension volunteers in the first Peace Corps group in India took over the management of a government-owned farm. Their purpose, like Marty Ross's, was demonstration. They introduced a new variety of wheat, fertilized and cultivated it well, and it grew magnificently. Farmers in the area came around to admire it, and the volunteers explained how the farmers' crops could be the same.

Just a week before harvesting, the sky blackened and a

violent hailstorm beat the volunteers' wheat into the ground. Only a fraction of it could be salvaged. In one of those inexplicable freaks of nature, their wheat field was the only one in the area to be damaged by the hail. The farmers took this as a clear sign from the gods that they should not raise that kind of wheat.

The next season the volunteers planted the same variety of wheat again. Although their two-year tours were up, they stayed on to take care of the wheat and harvest it. This time no hail came and the crop was bumper. The local farmers were impressed.

On June 12, 1963, Medgar Evers, a black civil rights worker, was ambushed and shot to death at his home in Jackson, Mississippi. When word of that cowardly act reached India, a black volunteer—one of the few in the country—came to our house one night. He was crying. He wanted to resign and go home to work for civil rights. What was he doing trying to help farmers in India, he asked me, when his people were being murdered in the United States? I didn't have a very good answer for him, but I didn't think he should resign; I thought it might always stay with him that he hadn't finished his job. I tried to convince him that he would have the rest of his life to work for civil rights once he returned to the States. We talked most of the night, and the next day he caught a bus and went back to his village. I have never been entirely sure that I gave him the right advice; I hope I did.

A shudder went through the Peace Corps on November 22, 1963, when news of President Kennedy's murder was flashed around the world. Of all New Frontier programs, the Peace Corps had drawn most heavily on Kennedy's charisma and his image. I think that almost every volunteer felt that in Peace Corps service he or she was giving the most tangible

95

and symbolic response to Kennedy's challenge, "Ask not what your country can do for you—ask what you can do for your country."

Kennedy's popularity in the developing countries of Africa, Asia, and Latin America was enormous, and volunteers basked in the esteem in which he was held. Volunteers from every country reported that for days after the assassination they were visited by friends and even by strangers who simply wanted to make a personal expression of their sadness at the President's death. Volunteers everywhere, often the only Americans in an area, were always known as symbols of one of Kennedy's dreams.

One volunteer in India told me that a farmer with whom he had been working for a year heard the news of Kennedy's death on the village radio. The farmer walked ten miles through an unseasonable rain to the volunteer's home to make sure that his young American friend had heard the tragic news and to express his sorrow.

Volunteers had been serving overseas less than two years at the time of Kennedy's death. In that time the program had become so firmly established that it moved on with a pause of respect and affection but without the slightest faltering from the course on which it was set. About 7,000 volunteers were serving overseas when Kennedy died. That number would more than double in the next three years. I'm sure Kennedy would have approved.

When Jack Vaughn replaced Shriver as head of the Peace Corps at the beginning of 1966, he made get-acquainted visits to several countries. One of his stops was in India, which at that time was the largest Peace Corps program in the world with more than seven hundred volunteers. I met Jack at the airport, of course, and when we came out, I was astonished to see fifty or more volunteers from the Delhi area gathered at the airport entrance. They had hired an elephant and his handler, and the elephant was decked out in festive fittings, including a howdah, the traditional chair-seat for honored passengers. The volunteers insisted that Jack and I ride part of the way back to Delhi on the back of the elephant.

Later that year Jack Vaughn called me back to Washington to be director of training. In 1967, when he was looking for a deputy director for the Peace Corps, he chose me. I have always thought the elephant ride from Palam Airport and the sparkle of the volunteers in India might have been in the back of Jack's mind when he made his choice.

# Washington and Beyond

I returned to a Washington absorbed in the drama of the great civil rights freedom struggle of the 1960s and almost in a state of shock over the protests against the war in Vietnam. I was pleased to see how Peace Corps volunteers, now returning by the thousands from two years of service overseas, were fitting into the turbulent national scene. Part of my time was spent in tracking their reentry and in seeing how or if the Peace Corps could help.

They really didn't need much help. One study we made of 10,000 returned volunteers showed that by far the largest number, over 37 percent, were continuing their education. Their Peace Corps years had shown them the need for maximum education to be effective in today's world. The evidence of career change was strong; a large number were preparing to be teachers in American schools.

In fact, an astonishing number, over 2,000—one out of every five in the 10,000 sample—were already teaching, many of them in urban slum and ghetto schools. The city of Philadelphia, desperate for teachers for its inner-city schools, queried the Peace Corps volunteer teachers in Africa who were finishing their tours in the summer of 1966 about their interest in teaching in Philadelphia. Over 175 volunteers signed and returned the contracts and were in the classrooms when school started in Philadelphia that fall.

Robert W. Blackburn, who handled this unusual experiment in recruitment for the city, later testified before a congressional committee that school officials in Philadelphia regarded the former Peace Corps volunteers as "the single best source of topflight educators available to us anywhere."

That was high praise.

The study of the 10,000 returned volunteers showed a sharp bent toward public service and social service jobs. Over 250 were working in President Johnson's new War on Poverty programs. Another 600 were in nonprofit health, labor, social service, and educational organizations. Almost 400 were employed by state and local governments. Four hundred were working on the Peace Corps staff, most of them overseas; 200 were working for the Agency for International Development, and 100 were in such international organizations as CARE and UNICEF.

The former volunteers were troubled by the America to which they had returned: the continuing injustices to racial minorities, the neglect of the poor, the rigidity of unresponsive government bureaucracy. But with few exceptions they rejected the routes of violence and destruction and the hippie route of withdrawal as avenues for taking up their life in America again. These men and women who had returned from the villages and slums of Africa, Asia, and Latin America had brought with them a commitment to service, and service is the opposite of destroying or withdrawing.

I think most volunteers, from their service overseas, learned a fundamental truth about the basic similarity of mankind: that the motives, aspirations, latent abilities, and behavior of peoples are really only superficially different as a result of the overlay of a particular culture. This deep-felt sense of our common humanity was—and is—a tremendous asset in approaching the problems of our country. A firm conviction that intrinsically people *are* equal is an important truth to have in one's intellectual arsenal.

The war in Vietnam divided America as no war had since the Civil War, and war protest was building to its highest level at the time I returned from India. From my office in the Peace Corps building I had a perfect view of the White House, just across Lafayette Square. Sometimes when I was working at night, I would stand at my office window and watch the long lines of candlelight marchers, moving silently past the White House. At other times antiwar rallies by tens of thousands of young men and women on the mall and around the Washington Monument were noisy and bitter.

We never took a count, of course, but I have no doubt that most Peace Corps volunteers opposed U.S. participation in the conflict in Vietnam. They felt—as did almost everyone else who opposed the war—that whether Vietnam became a Communist country was a matter for the Vietnamese to decide, that the United States had nothing to gain from fighting in Southeast Asia and no moral right to be there. They felt that the kinds of weapons we were using there—defoliants (Agent Orange), napalm, and massive aerial bombardment—were evil. In addition, almost every country in which Peace Corps volunteers served was critical of the United States' role in Vietnam. Volunteers were often accused of being a peace "decoy" for a country waging an immoral war.

I spent a considerable amount of time talking about Vietnam with volunteer groups in training and with volunteers overseas. The Peace Corps' position was that volunteers could exercise their freedom of speech all they wanted to in protesting the war as private citizens. We asked them not to protest as Peace Corps volunteers or in the name of the Peace Corps. That kind of protest always made news, and it embarrassed the U.S. government. I would say that my batting average in getting that point of view across was only fair.

My personal view was that we should not have been fighting a war in Vietnam, but I understood the opposing point of view. Beginning with Truman, every American president—Eisenhower, Kennedy, Johnson—had supported some kind of U.S. involvement in Vietnam. Millions of Americans strongly believed that our support of non-Communist South Vietnam was necessary to prevent the expansion of Communism in Southeast Asia. They thought that if Communist North Vietnam took over South Vietnam, other Southeast Asian countries such as Thailand, Indonesia, and the Philippines would topple like a row of dominoes in the face of advancing Communism. This belief was known as the domino theory.

What dismayed me was the way Vietnam veterans were treated when they returned to the United States. I served in a war where every returning veteran was treated like a hero, whether he was or not. In most cases, men and women who returned from the war in Vietnam were at best ignored; at worst they were looked down on and insulted. Thousands of Vietnam heroes came back not to a hero's welcome but to cold silence and even contempt. The Vietnam veterans' treatment was not only unworthy of a great nation, it was downright shameful. I knew it then; it became even clearer to me in the years after the war. One of the reasons I wrote *Always to Remember,* a book about the Vietnam Veterans Memorial in Washington, was that I could not get the shabby treatment of the men and women who fought in Vietnam out of my head.

Certain high-level jobs in the executive and judicial branches of government are called presidential appointments. The person who holds such a job is nominated directly by the president, then he or she must be confirmed in the job by the Senate as a part of that body's responsibility to "advise and consent" on appointments that the president wishes to make. All cabinet and supreme court positions are presidential appointments, of course. There are hundreds of much lower positions but still senior enough to require presidential appointment and confirmation by the Senate. The position of deputy director of the Peace Corps is one of those.

When the position of deputy director became vacant in 1967, Jack Vaughn went to President Johnson and told him that he would like for me to be his deputy. The embattled President, weighed down by war protests and facing the specter of having to send even more troops to Vietnam, had never heard of me and at that point couldn't give any real thought to the Peace Corps. When he came back from the White House, Jack told me that the President had asked just one question about me: "Is he loyal?" Jack assured President Johnson that I was.

Loyalty was not a problem for me. The civil rights struggle of American blacks reaching its apex in the sixties, I considered to be one of the historic pages in our nation's history and one of the very most important. President Johnson's record on civil rights stood above that of every president since Lincoln. Johnson had supported and signed into law the Civil Rights Act of 1964; his Great Society and War on Poverty programs were strongly directed toward furthering civil rights. I was 100 percent loyal to the President in this area. On Vietnam I would do what I could to keep volunteer war protests on a personal level.

Even in those grim and tense days in Washington, amusing things could happen. The time came when I had to appear before the Senate Foreign Relations Committee for my confirmation hearing as deputy director of the Peace Corps. I was nervous and crammed as full of Peace Corps facts and figures as an industrious staff had been able to cram me. Only a few members of the committee were present, and after some routine questioning they all left except the chairman, Senator William Fulbright. He looked over my résumé, saw that I had written some books, and commented on *The Lion's Whiskers,* which he thought was an eye-catching title.

We had a discussion about education in Africa and then the Senator returned to *The Lion's Whiskers.* "That certainly is an interesting title," he said. "I wish you would tell me about the book."

So to my complete amazement I spent most of my confirmation hearing telling African folktales to Chairman Fulbright, who seemed much more absorbed in these stories than he had been in all of the profound things I had to say about the Peace Corps.

The next day the full Senate confirmed my appointment as a routine piece of business.

When Richard Nixon was elected President, I submitted my resignation, as all presidential appointees are expected to do when a new President takes office. Three months later Nixon accepted my resignation, and I left the Peace Corps after what had been the richest, most exciting, most satisfying eight and a half years of my life. I told about those years in *A Moment in History,* which I wrote after I left the Peace Corps.

* * *

The Ashabranner family's roots quickly took hold in native soil once more when we returned to Washington in 1966. We lived in a nice home in Kensington, Maryland, a suburb of Washington. Melissa finished her senior year of high school and went to Temple University in Philadelphia where she received a degree in anthropology. She worked for a health services company in Washington for several years then continued her education at Yale University taking a master's degree in public and private management.

Melissa returned to Washington and married Jean-Keith Fagon, a charming and talented young man she had known for several years. Jean-Keith is Jamaican; he came to the United States to finish his education at Johns Hopkins University in Baltimore, then stayed on in Washington. Together Jean-Keith and Melissa have created a group of Washington community newspapers, the flagship of which, *The Hill Rag*, has been a major voice on Capitol Hill for over ten years. More important, they have given Martha and me the world's most beautiful grandson: Giancarlo Brent Fagon.

Jennifer finished high school, tried college and decided the academic life was not for her. Always a lover of dogs and cats, she went to a professional dog grooming school and became an expert groomer. Jennifer also had been interested in photography for years. She studied photography at nights and on weekends at the Northern Virginia Community College and at the Smithsonian Institution in Washington. She managed a photography laboratory for the Fairfax, Virginia, Recreational Program on weekends.

After a while Jennifer began taking photographs of dogs she had groomed and sold them to the dogs' doting owners. She now combines grooming and professional photography, having, as she says, the best of two worlds. Jennifer lives in

Alexandria, Virginia, just fifteen minutes from Melissa's house on Capitol Hill.

With Melissa and Jennifer going their separate and successful ways, Martha and I decided to return to the overseas life. I joined the Ford Foundation, America's largest philanthropic foundation, and we lived four years in the Philippines and four years in Indonesia in Southeast Asia. My job was to make educational grants to colleges and universities in those countries. Giving away money is fun but much harder work than it sounds.

After Indonesia, we returned home, this time to stay. We felt we had lived and worked overseas long enough, and I wanted to devote all my time, at long last, to writing. Now I had a good retirement income and no Depression-era hangups about job security. A full-time writer is what I have become, concentrating mainly but not exclusively on books about minorities and growing ethnic groups in America: Hispanics, Asians, Native Americans, and others. I believe that my years of living overseas have helped me to understand better their hopes, desires, frustrations, and fears. I really am a storyteller, just as I was when I began writing fifty years ago. The difference now is that I tell stories about real people who are trying to cope with very real and serious problems of living.

A few years ago Martha and I moved to Williamsburg, Virginia. This cradle of American democracy is a quiet and wonderfully rich place for me to write about my country, which is exactly what I want to do at this time in my life. A delightful bonus is that my family has been able to be a part of my life as a writer. Martha frequently travels with me, helps with interviews, sometimes takes photographs for my books and articles, and reads my manuscripts with a critical and practiced eye.

Melissa and I have collaborated on two books, *Into a Strange Land,* a book about unaccompanied refugee children in America, and *Counting America,* the story of the United States census and its importance. She is very busy with her newspapers, but we hope to write more together. Jennifer has taken the photographs for three of my books: *Always to Remember,* the book about the Vietnam Veterans Memorial; *Crazy About German Shepherds;* and *A Grateful Nation,* which is the story of Arlington National Cemetery. *Crazy About German Shepherds* was really Jennifer's idea, and we want to do some more dog books together.

I have lived long enough and seen enough of the world to know what a fortunate man I am.

# *Some Thoughts About the Future*

T he concerns of the United States on which I am not an expert would make a long list; among them would be the proliferation of nuclear weapons, the environment, drugs, and our national debt. But my life and work have made me—if not an expert—at least well informed on two subjects that I think are important for all Americans.

As America heads into the twenty-first century, we should be glad that we have a foreign assistance agency—the Agency for International Development—and a Peace Corps that have stood the test of time. The Peace Corps today is strong and well run. The volunteers are as dedicated, tough, imaginative, and well motivated as they ever were. There have been some changes since the 1960s. Volunteers are a bit older now, and most of them are somewhat better qualified in terms of job skills. About half of all Peace Corps volunteers today are women, a much higher percentage than in my time. All of these changes are good. With more than 6,000 volunteers overseas, the Peace Corps is still large enough to make a difference.

Most of the countries of Africa, Asia, and Latin America remain poor, desperately poor. Once we thought that the conditions that cause poverty in these countries could be corrected in a few years; now we know the necessary changes will take a long time. But we must keep trying, not only for the sake of the people in those countries but for our own sake as well. The poverty of Africa, Asia, and Latin America threatens the security of the rest of the world. The rich, industrialized nations of the world cannot hope to wall themselves off and pretend that the poor nations do not exist. Their poverty will mean grief for everyone.

Fortunately, the United States is by no means the only country helping the poor developing countries today. Most European countries as well as Canada, Australia, and Japan now have foreign aid programs. Some of these countries spend a greater percentage of their national income on such programs than the United States does. They know, as we do, that the fight against world poverty will be a long and sometimes frustrating one but that it must be fought.

The idea that rich nations might use some of their wealth and knowledge to help poor nations achieve a better life for their people is one of the great breakthrough concepts of history. We should be glad that it is an idea of our time.

Racism and ethnic hatred are the most abiding and pernicious ills of mankind. I saw abundant evidence of both in every country we lived in. In Ethiopia some tribes were looked down on because they were "blacker" than other tribes. In Nigeria, Ibos, Hausas, and Yorubas, the large ethnic groups of the country, fought each other in a disastrous civil war in the sixties. Bloody conflict continues to take place in India between Hindus and Muslims and between Hindus and Sikhs; although the caste system has been outlawed in India, I was in villages where "untouchables" were scorned by everyone else and could not even use the same wells that other people used. In the Philippines, Muslims fought Christians; in Indonesia, the Chinese minority suffered brutal oppression in the sixties, and discrimination continues against Chinese in Indonesia as well as in some other Southeast Asian countries.

Clearly, America has no monopoly on racism and ethnic discrimination. But we do have both, and continuing the struggle against them should be at the top of our national agenda. We have made progress. I find it hard to believe that during a considerable part of my life schools were legally segregated by race, that because of their color some people had to ride in the back of the bus, could not eat in certain restaurants, could not use certain public restrooms, could not buy houses in certain parts of town, could not participate in professional sports, could not attend universities that their own tax dollars were helping to support, were segregated in military service, had no hope of fair or equal treatment when seeking jobs in the marketplace.

The great breakthroughs in civil rights came from the freedom struggles of the 1960s that were led by courageous black Americans and were supported by white Americans who wanted to see a shameful social system end. But much more needs to be done to bring about a full and equal participation in American society by blacks and other minorities. More needs to be done in providing educational opportunities, job opportunities, housing opportunities. Perhaps we need a Marshall Plan for the inner cities of America.

The world exists as it does because of the way we think

about each other. Until people change the way they think about other people—and only education in all its forms can eventually bring that change—we must have laws to protect human and civil rights. The civil rights laws that we now have in America have been hard won and are precious. We must protect them against the ever-present danger of erosion.

# *Bibliography*

In writing this memoir I have consulted the following publications, some of them my own, to refresh my memory about events, names, dates, and places.

Ashabranner, Brent. *A Moment in History: The First Ten Years of the Peace Corps.* Garden City, New York: Doubleday & Company, Inc., 1971.

Blumberg, Rhoda Lois. *Civil Rights: The 1960s Freedom Struggle.* Boston: Twayne Publishers, 1984.

Costello, John. *The Pacific War.* New York: Rawson, Wade Publishers, 1981.

Davis, Russell and Brent Ashabranner. "Harvesting Folk Tales." *The Horn Book Magazine,* April, 1960.

——. *The Lion's Whiskers: Tales of High Africa.* Boston: Little, Brown and Company, 1959.

——. *Point Four Assignment.* Boston: Little, Brown and Company, 1959.

Lindop, Edmund. *The Turbulent Thirties.* New York: Franklin Watts, Inc., 1970.

Mee, Charles L., Jr. *The Marshall Plan.* New York: Simon and Schuster, 1984.

Paradis, Adrian A. *The Hungry Years: The Story of the Great American Depression*. New York: Chilton Book Company, 1967.

Ryan, Michael. "Should the Peace Corps Survive?" *Parade Magazine*, April 1, 1990.

Settel, Irving. *A Pictorial History of Radio*. New York: Grosset & Dunlap, 1960, 1967.

Steinberg, Rafael. *Island Fighting*. Alexandria, Virginia: Time-Life Books, 1978.

# *Index*